David Lampe
Ithaca
Feb. '88

Oxbridge Blues
and Other Stories

Oxbridge Blues
and Other Stories

Frederic Raphael

University of Arkansas Press
Fayetteville, 1984

Library of Congress Cataloging in Publication Data

Raphael, Frederic, 1931–
  Oxbridge blues and other stories.

  Selections from the author's Oxbridge blues and
Sleeps six and other stories.
  I. Raphael, Frederic, 1931–   . Sleeps six and
other stories. Selections. II. Title.
PR6068.A6A6 1984   823'.914   83-18268
ISBN 0-938626-27-2
ISBN 0-938626-28-0 (pbk.)

The stories in this collection were included in two
volumes of Frederic Raphael's work published in
England by Jonathan Cape under the titles *Oxbridge
Blues* (1980) and *Sleeps Six and Other Stories* (1979).

Contents

Also by Frederic Raphael

Fiction

April, June and November
California Time   *The Earlsdon Way*
The Glittering Prizes (1976 series)
Like Men Betrayed   *The Graduate Wife*
The Limits of Love   *Lindmann*
Orchestra and Beginners
Oxbridge Blues   *Richard's Things*
Sleeps Six   *The Trouble with England*
Who Were You with Last Night?
A Wild Surmise

Screenplays

Darling
Far from the Madding Crowd
Two for the Road
W. Somerset Maugham and His World

Translations

The Oresteia of Aeschylus (with Kenneth McLeish)
The Poems of Catullus (with Kenneth McLeish)

Nonfiction

Bookmarks (editor)   *Byron*
Cracks in the Ice: Criticism of Two Decades
— *The List of Books* (with Kenneth McLeish)

A Travel Note

A share of the attraction these stories hold for an American reader lies in the Britishness of them. Such a reader, once inside them, is no longer in New York or Atlanta or Denver, but in England, where American is not spoken. The world would seem skewed if we found the people of London talking like the people of Cincinnati, so we have left the British spellings as they come to us; the pronunciation seems at times to be heard through them.

If some words seem strange, or strangely used, to the ear of the American reader, they seem that way also at first to the ear of an American traveler. They nearly always become clear in context: "public schools" are private schools, a "boot" is a car's trunk, a "bonnet" is its hood, "removal men" are furniture movers, a "Brummy" is a man from Birmingham, a "dottle" is the plug of half-burnt tobacco in the bottom of a pipe bowl, a policeman's "patch" is his beat, "F.T." is the *Financial Times*, and a "zebra" is a crosswalk. Welcome to England. With a side trip to Spain.

Similar Triangles

It was not a cosy, modern adultery. There was much anguish in it. They spoke sometimes, lying in afternoon shadows in borrowed or hired beds, of the long cost of the thing, in pain and deception. They were confident that their spouses knew nothing of the passion which, with irregular regularity, hurried them, hot, across town to hastily scribbled, then crumpled, rendezvous. Their affair had its own narrow and precise language; after each meeting, his mistress would clip a single curl of hair, in the Italian fashion, from *that* part of herself. Byron to her Teresa Guiccioli, he kept those black and glistening hairs, softly crepitant, in a self-addressed envelope in his bottom drawer at the office. They never wrote to each other. Their ordinary lives were happy with homes and cheerful with children; the durable shoe of marriage pinched but slightly and they scarcely noticed their wedded blisters. He had respect for her husband, a coeval at university, whose boring business luckily took him abroad every now and again; she was flattered by the beauty of his wife, whose vanity kept her unsuspicious, but whose looks, it was evident, did not entirely satisfy him.

The lovers would sometimes talk, as they wondered, naked, where their temporary host kept his tea these days, of their own one-day-perhaps marriage. They held the prospect enticingly ahead of themselves, donkeys who dangled their own carrot, but they were sensitive people and why should they hurt Tom or, for that matter, Rachel? They settled, with stimulating resignation, for the *status quo*, though privately she

1

could not but think that her condition was more painful than his. Her sentimental education had been founded on French models, though more on Beauvoir, she liked to think, than on Bovary. While she agreed to clip the triangular hedge of her sex to suit his topiaristic taste, she took sour pleasure in the belief that her love was more profound than his. He, for his part, salted his sweet wounds with the fear that she and Tom were really closer than he and she. His Narcissism saw itself in triple mirrors.

He was a rising civil servant, discreet to a fault, wise to a virtue. One day, just as he was about to go in to see his Master, whose latest Bill was being mauled in Committee, his secretary buzzed. His mistress seldom called him at the office and he raised the receiver with fond vexation. She was sorry to do this, but her husband had been at a conference at an out-of-season resort on the Bay of Naples and had been knocked down by a lorry full of soldiers. He begged leave from his understanding, displeased Minister, who hated all private life, and dashed into Whitehall for a cab. As he was driven across town, the unwanted comedy of his rival having been killed by, of all unlikely forces, the Italian army twisted his lips into a grin he had positively to manipulate into condolence.

But if he had sometimes wondered whether he truly loved his mistress, her tears soon washed away all doubts. In the unusual surroundings of her mournful house, he talked to her for the first time with a tenderness unspiked by desire. His wife was as generous as he had expected—the couples were amiable strangers—and, hearing that he had been the first on the scene, insisted that he stay and do anything he could. For the first time, he spent a whole night under the same roof as his mistress. Of course it was unthinkable that they make love. In the succeeding, painful days, tact continued to tailor modest skirts to a love whose shamelessness had always been its badge.

She had no idea that he could be so practical and so considerate. The children adored him. No one questioned his compassionate presence; neither her friends nor his, even when they were identical, passed the smallest sly observation. They hid their love in the open, and none remarked it.

Their desire had always before been a matter of urgent opportunism; its fervour was a function of its haste. Now decision was required to revive it. Neither doubted that it would come promptly when wanted, but they hesitated before pressing the bell. A week after the funeral, they sat one evening in the orange basement kitchen, among the blue-hooped dishes, while her daughter practised the clarinet upstairs and the au pair girl called out 'Goodnight then' as she set off to meet her Italian waiter, on his night off from the *trattoria* where he told show biz people how nice it was to see them again. They discussed the future and the past; they toyed, as with a new diet, with the idea of telling Rachel. When they did indeed come to make love again—the children at their grandmother's for a day or two—there was between them a certain gentle constraint; they told themselves it was because it now meant so much more than it had before. Yet he was kinder than was quite congenial to him; she was more touched, she found, than roused. And afterwards, she omitted, as if by mutual, mature consent, the ceremonial snip.

She understood, of course, of course she did, when he felt obliged to revert, at least for a while, to his familiar style of living. Rachel had been so terribly nice, I mean, hadn't she? His mistress was surprised, however, at how abruptly rare his calls became. How could he confess to her his unwanted and inexpressible dismay at the suddenly enlarged emptiness in his mistress's life or his unwillingness, his inability to fill it? She started to complain of his neglect and never heard the ugly tune she sang in her lover's ear.

In brief, though at length, he became inexorably, remorsefully, estranged from the woman with whom he had for so long dreamed of sharing his life, if only she were free. Resentment did not exorcise her love; truth to tell, his display of decent maturity had been rather unexciting. His new indifference promised that the old beastliness was not, after all, gone in him. She smiled, as she wept, at his cruelty. Friends saw that she was missing Tom badly and were kind in his stead: her evenings, if not her afternoons, were quickly filled. She dined out and soon she met a very nice man. Within a year she had married him. Her lover read the announcement and swore to himself that he would never see her again. But one evening, sullen with his sullen wife, he did see her, and the new husband, at a concert. During the Albinoni, he observed, in the calm possessive glance her husband slyly gave her, how much he resembled the dead Tom. A few days later, he called her during his Minister's question time. She told him, of course, how very happy she was with her new husband and he, of course, told her how happy he was that she was happy. Ned was a lawyer, she said, involved with the Common Market; he was quite often away for a day or so in Brussels or Strasbourg. Love and desire rose in grateful resurrection. When he proposed that they have lunch one day, she was reliably on cue: 'I say, can you get the flat, do you think?' Guilt returned to his life like spring. In very little time, the pattern was restored, as in a play which falters when a key actor has to be replaced, but which soon, when the casting is right, resumes its unfaltering rhythm.

Once again he did not have to say goodnight to the au pair off to her Italian or to smile at Clara's clarinet. Once again, in those brief brackets of infinity in which their passion had to be compressed, the deep and constricted flood of desire turned love's secret mill. Once again, with that old lost smile, she came to the borrowed bed with a pair of glinting nail scissors which, bending naked, she put on the bedside table, next to the telephone they always left unanswered if it rang, for the eventual climactic snip. Once again, his wife came to believe what she had sullenly begun to doubt, that he did indeed still find her beautiful.

Still Life

They worked for the same newspaper. She helped to edit the fashion pages; he was an erstwhile lawyer who specialised in economic news. Both were married, happily they promised each other when they first stood beside the broad bed, with its lemon-coloured sheets, which the dramatic critic kept for first nights. If the affair had begun out of a feeling that, at their ages, it was absurd to be faithful to marriages which had been going on so long, it soon became a kind of controlled obsession. Each, after all, had the children to think about and the present situation suited them both. She was fond enough of her husband, whose main fault was that he collaborated on comedy scripts with a man called Ronald. Ronald was always at their place and he called her 'lovey'. He valued his wife for the patience she showed to their middle child, who was fat and garrulous on account of some congenital defect neither money nor drugs could correct.

It pleased them to conduct their affair entirely in the West End. They never spent a whole night together. The secrecy, even the haste, with which they were obliged to make love spiced their desire. They ate in restaurants where he had entertained financiers for lunch. (He specialised in collecting spilled beans in return for quite a decent house claret and a duck thing they do rather well here.) It gratified him to be with a fashionable woman; his wife was much too sensible to wear those sorts of things, and in any case they hadn't really got the money, had they? The affair had begun with good humour. 'If this doesn't work,' they promised each other, 'we won't let it worry us.' Even when they had become regular lovers, there was something provisional in their passion.

One summer, when it had been going on for over a year, she told him that she was taking a holiday with her husband (thank God no Ronald!) and the two girls, in a farmhouse they had been lent by some friends in the Gorges du Tarn. 'That's really amazing,' he said, when he heard the address, 'because we've taken a cottage that can't be more than a dozen miles from where you're going to be!' 'Fate's at work,' she said, in that voice which seemed to mimic some unknown butt. He loved the slight jogging of her foot as she sat, one glistening leg crossed over the other. The slim slipper dangled from her nylon heel and inside he could just see the maker's gilded name, scarcely yet trodden upon. 'We must on no account meet,' she said. Yet the possibility that they might glimpse each other while engaged on some summer errand could not fail to enchant them. If only, by the way, they were going together. Imagine!

The holidays came. He could not help watching out for her when he went on the Saturday to the local town, efficient with his wife's neat shopping list. She was doing a chicken *à l'estragon* for lunch and hoped he didn't mind marketing alone. The kids were sick of the car and had gone up to see a new-born calf at the farm. He walked around the stalls, pretending to be as French as possible to keep the prices down, ears eager for English voices. Could that be her behind those dangling ducks, in the headscarf and the Woking accent? Of course not. On the way back to the cottage, he drove slightly out of his way and saw the signpost leading to the village featured in her address, but refrained from turning off.

Then, in the week, he took the family to the swimming pool near a mill where they had had some particularly good salmon trout the previous evening. He left them, on some cultural excuse, and drove away. It was not far to the village he had seen indicated. Though it contained only a few houses (two deserted), he had to ask an old woman, who was topping and tailing a colander of beans, which of the various tracks led to 'Les Pechs'. 'Le monsieur est sorti,' she said, in her harsh local accent. He started the car again hurriedly. If it was true that only the Monsieur had gone out, she might be there alone. The old lady would not have said if the children had gone with their father.

The farmhouse was an ancient building, opportunistically renovated with patches of beige concrete, its thick walls pierced with ready-made french windows. He knocked, but there was no answer. He tapped again on the locked kitchen door with a pebble, to sharpen the sound. Might she be upstairs? He cupped his hands and peered between them into the sun-splashed room. Used plates, badged with unfinished egg, were still on the table. He looked at his watch. It was four-fifteen. He looked again; a plastic bowl of overboiled potatoes already turning black; next to it, a ripped packet of chocolate biscuits and by them broken bread, a knob of butter and a jar of British jam, still open, a sticky-handled knife stuck in its strawberry wound. Curled ham and a segment of cold pizza, scabby with tomato, were exposed, in creased wrapping paper, to the flies. One of the kitchen chairs was on its back, as if it had passed out. In the corner of the room was a gaping suit-case; toys, anoraks and packets of cereal had been dug out and lay in a spoiled heap beside it.

He went back to the car and turned it in the awkward lane. He went too fast down the ruts back to the village and nodded at the old lady, who had finished her beans, before going on, more placidly, towards the main road. He had scarcely got there when a Volvo station wagon, unmistakably G.B., came towards him, slowing down. He looked and, sure enough, there she was, commonplace with her humorist husband and the growing girls. The latter, seeing another

English number plate, pressed their faces against the badges and cross-Channel stickers on the side window. 'Ullo, ullo,' they mouthed, lips moistening the dusty glass. He gave a little wave, and mouthed back, 'Goodbye, goodbye!'

Aperitif

'Yes,' she said, 'this is the place. I knew it was.'

'You came here with him, did you?'

'Twice,' she said. 'We came here twice. I recognise the lettering. It's more faded now, of course, but I remember it distinctly. We came here first on our honeymoon. The bed was hell.'

'It wasn't the first time you slept together, though, surely?'

'Oh good heavens no,' she said. 'I was pregnant with Nicholas. But not very. We had room number 7. The key was very stiff in the lock.'

'Suitably symbolic!' he said.

'Of what? Oh I see. We never had any trouble in that department as a matter of fact.'

'Pregnant with Nicholas,' he said. 'That certainly makes it quite a long time ago. Why, that must be—'

'Let's not bother to be precise, shall we?' she said.

'I hope Nicholas and I are going to be able to work out a modus vivendi,' he said. 'Of course I appreciate it isn't going to be easy.'

'In the final analysis,' she said, 'what is?'

'Personally,' he said, 'I always hope it won't *get* to the final analysis. It's almost certain to be too far. What's the food like?'

'If it's the same people, excellent. The *écrevisses* are sensational. I don't remember having better food anywhere. Although the first time I hardly ate anything. It is the same people! Bonjour, Madame Rigaud!'

'Madame. Monsieur.'

'Nous voudrions une chambre, s'il vous plaît—'

'Je regrette: nous ne faisons plus de chambres.'

"They don't do rooms any more? But it says hotel!'

'Je suppose que nous pouvons dîner, quand même, madame?'

'Mais oui. Vous n'êtes que deux?'

'Que deux,' he said.

'J'enlève le troisième couvert.'

'Do you think she recognised me? I thought she looked at me as if she had some idea—'

'When was the last time you were here?'

'About eight years ago,' she said. 'We left Nicholas and Hannah with the grandparents and had a trip on our own. It was rather a disaster. It was meant to repair things and it turned out to be rather a disaster. That's why I remember the place so well. We had an awful quarrel.'

'After you'd eaten, I presume.'

'Why?'

'Because the first time you hardly ate anything, you said, and yet you say the food's so good. So presumably you ate well the second time and had the row afterwards.'

'Aren't you logical?' she said.

'Why do you think there's no one else in the dining room?' he said. 'I hope it doesn't mean they've lost their chef.'

'As it's the same lady, and she's married to the chef, I don't think it's very likely.'

'You're the same lady,' he said, 'but you're not still married to the chef.'

'Michael was a good critic of cooking,' she said, 'but he didn't do any.'

'I was merely suggesting—'

'She looks older, she looks older and rather sadder.'

'That's what looking older is.'

'Oh do you think so?' she said. 'I rather hoped one got rather more—what?—characterful as one got older.'

'What did you quarrel about?' he said.

'It was rather funny, actually.'

'You'd rather not talk about it.'

'Oh I don't mind,' she said. 'I don't propose to have any secrets from you.'

'That makes it sound as if there are lots you could have.'

'What was funny was that we quarrelled about something that happened the first time. And it must have been—oh—almost ten years between the two visits.'

'Would you rather not talk about him?'

'Would you rather I didn't?'

'You don't find it morbid?'

'I don't mind a little morbidity,' she said, 'from time to time. Why do you suppose they don't do rooms any more?'

'Staff, I presume,' he said.

'It's rather like a ghost story,' she said. 'As if someone died, or was murdered or something. The first time we came we'd been driving all day. It was a bit foggy and we'd picked this place out, because it had a star for the restaurant, earlier in the day, before the weather turned foul. I said we should stop somewhere else, but you know how obstinate he could be. He wanted to come here and he said he could get us here and we drove and we drove. It was obviously going to be hellishly late when we got here, but he was determined.'

'I can imagine.'

'Yes, and by the time we did get here, I had absolutely no appetite at all. I was past it, I suppose. I felt sick. He made me drink some champagne, but it only made me feel worse, and then he was annoyed because he was stuck with the bottle and I didn't want any more.'

'Quite natural in the circumstances.'

'Oh perfectly. Don't imagine I'm criticising. Anyway, I said he should eat before it was too late, even though I didn't want to, so we both came into the dining room, even though I really couldn't face the thought of food, let alone the sight of it—'

'I say, I wish they'd bring us the menu.'

'They probably don't start till half past—and there was another couple sitting in here, just one, finishing their rasp- berries. Over there. Michael took one look at them and blushed like a schoolboy. A middle-aged man and his rather dowdy wife. They didn't mean a thing to me. Well, it turned out that he was a don from Michael's old college.'

'Extraordinary coincidence!'

'Yes. He didn't seem particularly pleased to see Michael. They hadn't had anything in common at Cambridge—the man was an archaeologist or a geologist or something—and I don't suppose he was particularly glad to hear English spoken at all, let alone be accosted and introduced to some ex-undergradu- ate's wife. He said hullo and they finished their raspberries and said they'd take their coffee later, when they'd had a bit of a stroll. Michael bobbed up again from his chair as they went out and said perhaps we could all have a brandy together afterwards. The archaeologist or whatever he was didn't give that idea more than about three out of ten, but he said perhaps and out they went. Michael went on eating and then he said, "I suppose I should have said cognac. Not brandy." And I said I didn't really think he should have said anything at all.'

'You were a bitch even then.'

'I didn't say it bitchily. You've got me completely wrong if you think that. I smiled. Don't think I didn't love Michael at that point. I loved him very much.'

'I know that.'

'Anyway, I was feeling a bit better. I had some of Michael's chicken and I rather wanted to get him upstairs to bed, as a matter of fact. Well, after dinner he ordered coffee and generally rather dawdled about and I realised he was hoping that this don of his was going to come back and have this famous brandy. Eventually I said I was going up, if he didn't mind, and he decided he might as well come too. They must have slipped up to bed themselves or something. So up we went.'

'And how did it go?'

'What? Oh, the sex. Very well. Probably the belated effect of the champagne. Though Michael and I rarely had problems in that department.'

'Then what was the row about?'

'The row was ten years later.'

'But presumably something happened?'

'Ten years later. After dinner.'

'Of course. I say I do wish she'd at least bring us a menu.'

'Madame insisted on showing us her *Livre d'Or*. You know, her distinguished visitors' book. I suppose Michael looked sufficiently haggard to deserve an entry or something.'

'Why did Michael get to look like that?'

'Being married to me,' she said. 'Why don't you ask me a difficult one?'

'You're beautiful,' he said. 'That's not always easy to handle, is it, in wives?'

'Anyway, there in the book—when we looked back, you know how one does—was the signature of this don of Michael's. And he'd written this elaborately effusive nonsense about the hotel and about how it had been recommended to him by a wiser and a better man, some professor or other he obviously wanted to oil up to, and so on and so on. Well, I just burst out laughing. It was absolutely ludicrous. And that was it. Michael was furious. I couldn't believe it. He was livid. He said I'd been absurdly jealous and bad-mannered and it was no wonder that they'd never come and had their brandy with us—'

'Their cognac—'

'Their cognac, whatever it was—because I'd been so graceless it was embarrassing. I said I'd had a headache and I'd done the best I could and—well, you can imagine—'

'Easily,' he said. 'Ten years later, this was?'

'Yes,' she said, 'and he went on about how I'd always resented his Cambridge friends. It all developed from that. I said he was hopelessly fixated or why did he care so much about the drinking company of some stupid, overweight don who obviously didn't want to be bothered with him anyway?'

'I can imagine how it ended.'

'I can't remember which one of us it was,' she said, 'but of course eventually one of us had to say that it was a pity we'd had to wait ten years and two children and God knows what before we discovered that in the final analysis we absolutely despised each other.'

'You see?' he said. 'The final analysis. That's why I profoundly hope we never have one. Ah, here she comes. You're sure you don't mind eating here in the circumstances?'

'No,' she said, 'as a matter of fact it's given me quite an appetite. Telling you all that.'

'Me too,' he said, 'me too. Poor old Michael. Pity they don't still have rooms.'

Benchmark

His father had been a barrister and it seemed only natural that he should read for the Bar. He was clever; he might have been anything and so all decision seemed to him at once temporary and arbitrary. Versatility made him docile. As he counted up to forty the quota of dutiful dinners at his father's Inn, it amused him to think of himself as a dangerous monster, blessed (or was it cursed?) with three eyes. Unless he concealed his extraordinary gift, the crowd might become aware of it, and turn on him. He developed a habit of putting his hand over his forehead when talking or arguing. It is said to be in the middle of his forehead that man once carried that third and terrible eye. You can still feel the dip of the socket.

He was, in all observable respects, a normal and intelligent young man of his time. At the university he was known for his sometimes savage mimicry of personalities of the day, but by the time he had finished his dinners and, thus fortified, was approaching his Bar Finals, he had ceased to imitate anyone but the striped-trousered, stiff-collared young devilling junior he proposed to become.

One day, at a party overlooking the river by Turner's Reach, he met a girl. The flat was very grand; it belonged to a rich business man whom his father had extricated from some taxing trouble. It was so big that it contained a fountain. He was floating a frilly garter from a cold lamb chop in the throbbing water when he met the woman whom he would marry, and who would marry him. She was dark, with a long face, beautiful enough to be painted and distinct enough to

15

be caricatured. She wore a black silk dress, no jewellery. Her hair was in a bun, swollen, yet firmly contained; it was lustrous, the dark hair, and seemed to pulse with life, as if it were flesh, as if it had nerves and, when touched, would flinch or flower. She was recently down from Oxford; she had read English. Her father was the business man. She disdained the law, as beauty may, and was not impressed by the brilliance of his results so far. And so, as if to disclose his third and magic eye, he told her that he sometimes wrote poetry. Her eyes lost their cataracts of contempt. Did he have any of his poems with him? He did not, and was glad, for now it was easy to find a reason to meet again.

They did so in the Criterion restaurant, where crustless triangular sandwiches and a choice of tea cakes were once wheeled on trolleys under a gilded mosaic ceiling. Now the ceiling alone remained, a golden heaven above a mundane modernised earth: the place had been converted to self-service. Fish and chips and individual fruit pies had ousted cucumber sandwiches and creamily tumescent éclairs. She wore a tweed skirt this time and a sweater that was both green and blue. She put on a pair of glasses and swallowed and began to read his verses.

'Well, what do you think?' She looked from the pages in her hand to his face, and back again, as if seeking a likeness. She rested the poems in her herringboned lap and leaned forward over a steeple of white-knuckled fingers. 'I think I love you,' she said. 'About the poems,' he said. 'I like them,' she said, 'a lot.' 'But are they any good?' 'I think they're very good,' she said, 'do you?' 'I write poems,' he said, 'but whether or not I'm a poet ... ' She smiled — oh that red unreddened mouth! — and the steeple came suddenly down. 'That's a critical question, isn't it?' she said, and laid a long hand on his.

She was a virgin, but she was promptly moist for him, as if she had already known men. He wanted to marry her; she intended to marry him. By day he worked for his Finals, behaved as correctly as ever and aped, with the skill he had always contrived, the ways of the pedestrian world. He knew she was rich and he was fired with ambition to give her everything she had already. He was ready to give his life for that. Their desire was so strong and, to them, so reckless that it seemed as necessary as it was delicious to hide its pulse under commonplace clothing. They married and they were lovers. He became an advocate of mordant effectiveness: his bite rewardingly worse than his bark. He relished the polite mercilessness of legal debate; it particularly pleased him to be known as an expert on matters of which, until the eve of a case, he knew virtually nothing.

His marriage was at first his passion, then his delight, later his pleasure and always his comfort. His wife continued to excite both his desire and his admiration, even when they had been married for more than twenty years and their children had lovers of their own. (His son did not want to go to the Bar; he was a garage mechanic and wore a dog collar and a gold ear-ring in his left ear.) His wife was as publicly assured as she could still be privately demanding. She dressed as the wife of a fashionable Q.C. should, and her cocktail parties were unostentatiously showy: nothing was too much trouble and nothing appeared to have been any trouble at all. The ham and the smoked salmon—where did she get them?—came from a famous, known-to-few smokery near their cottage on the east coast. Soon after their silver wedding anniversary, he was made a judge. He was knighted, in happy consequence, and his wife enjoyed the embarrassment of being her ladyship. They celebrated in bed; public position lending piquancy to private.

As a result of his elevation, he had to vacate his chambers, which had belonged to his father and were crammed with ancient, jaundiced papers. He was already installed on the Chancery bench before he had completed the job. He was somewhat dismayed to find that he did not in the least like being a judge: it was tedious and it was lonely. He sat for long periods, properly attentive, with his hand over his forehead. He felt himself to be concealing that third eye in the centre of his brow which already saw, and too clearly, where the whole thing was leading.

He had quite forgotten about his adolescent poetry and was astonished to come across a batch of it at the bottom of a cupboard. He smiled—golly!—at the sight of it and took it out and started to read, for a laugh. He expected clinching evidence of the folly of youthful pretensions. His whole happy life had been founded on the assumption that he had been right to abdicate before his wife's gentle, unmistakable judgment. He sat on the floor of his chambers, boyishly grey, and prepared to be embarrassed by these unburnt embers. Instead, the poems passed sentence on his life. At last, he closed his eyes to escape their indictment, but the unblinking eye in the centre of his forehead gazed and blazed with unique and undeniable vision. He cowered on the floor of the dusty cave and saw that the years of his life had escaped, like Odysseus' men under the panicky sheep of the blind, deluded Polyphemus. 'Who are you, who are you?' he cried. And the voice of the man who had blinded himself replied, 'No one. No one.'

Cheap Day

Every three or four weeks there came a moment when, as she would say to her husband at breakfast, she simply had to go up to town. She had been born in London; her mother lived there; she had friends, the dentist, and things to do. She had come to love the estuary, the open skies, the smell of the mud-stained sea, but every three or four weeks she simply had to go up to town. 'Why do it if you don't want to?' her husband would ask. 'You go sometimes,' she answered. 'But I want to,' he said.

There was a new car park at the station, into which com-muters' cars could pass only one at a time. Seasoned travellers had taken all the spaces near the booking office and she was constrained, in her camel-hair suit, with its rather narrow skirt, to hurry on foot from the back of the old coal-yard, where late traffic was driven to park, along the cold rows of early cars, uneasy on her higher-than-usual heels. The London train was already chattering into the station as she stood pant-ing at the booking office. A cheap day ticket was placed on the little bisected turntable and rotated to her. She ran down the stairs, through mottled puddles and along the long platform from which, thank God, belted bundles of old Sunday supple-ments were being loaded onto the train. There was plenty of time and she would not really mind, she promised herself, if she didn't go to London anyway, and yet she ran.

She grabbed open the door of an apparently empty non-smoker. A man in a brown corduroy jacket and fawn trousers was crouched down collecting a jumble of papers from the floor and posting them in the mouth of his rigid briefcase. 'Sorry,' he said breathlessly, 'but I've been an absolute idiot and opened my briefcase the wrong way up.' 'I shouldn't worry,' she gasped. 'Oh,' he said, 'you've been running too.' 'Isn't it too silly,' she said, 'when we still haven't even left the station?' 'You didn't stop to buy a ticket, did you?' He had noticed the tab of cheap paper in her gloved fingers. 'I'm always afraid of being accused of doing something wrong,' she said.

The train was soon moving through flat fields and then alongside the by-pass where they could measure their pace against shirt-sleeved salesmen who were proving that their company cars had effective heaters, and how far they had come in them. Frost still made mountainous birthday cakes out of molehills in the meadows. 'I hate to run for things, don't you?' he said, as he felt for his pencil. 'And yet one does it,' she said. 'One does so many things one doesn't want to do, and so few one does,' he said, 'why is that, do you suppose?' 'Perhaps one isn't sure which is which,' she said. She had neither a book nor a paper. He looked up at her from the things in his lap. 'For instance, I should dearly like to tell you what remarkable eyes you have, but the habit of reticence is, of course, much too strong to admit of such impertinence.' 'Do you often talk to women like that in trains?' As she recovered her breath, youth came back into her face, defeating time. 'I'll tell you the truth,' he said, 'never. But to act out of character is to escape, if only for a moment, from the human condition. Don't you agree?' 'I think you talk to women in trains quite a bit,' she said.

He made a mark on the print in front of him. 'I've been visiting my ex-wife,' he said, 'and the children. Perhaps that's what's responsible. She left me for another man—not that I was blameless—and then he was killed in one of those holiday air crashes. Forty-fourth out of a list of forty-six victims; he was on business, the rest of them weren't. Much it mattered; Ginny was left with virtually nothing.' 'And you help her?'

'Of course.' 'But you never got back together?' 'It's as if there were a sort of membrane between us,' he said, 'thin and invisible but terribly durable—a man-made fibre, no doubt—and we can never quite breach it; *hymen hymenaeo*, the moment is never quite propitious.' 'Are you a don, by any chance, or a lecturer?' 'I used to be a schoolmaster,' he said, pencil against page, 'but now I compile reference books and things. What makes you ask?' 'Propitious,' she said, and crossed blue-stockinged legs.

As they careered through a station, their view was hedged with the blurred faces of local passengers, waiting for the next train. 'We travel at different speeds from each other,' he said, 'and so are prevented from joining those with whom we should dearly like to travel.' 'Isn't that the reason we imagine we'd like to travel with them?' she said. 'Look here,' he said, 'may I ask you something: what are you doing this morning, when we get to town, and are you free for lunch by any chance?' 'I've got my mother,' she said. 'Well, what about before?' 'And rather a full morning,' she said, 'I'm afraid. I go up to town only once or so a month and—' 'Why are you afraid?' 'It's only a manner of speaking,' she said, 'I'm not actually all that afraid—' 'I never supposed you were. What about coffee? It's only eleven.' 'I've got to go and see a cousin of mine who's in hospital. The Royal Free. You don't happen to know where it is exactly by any chance, do you?' 'The Royal Free,' he said, 'that sounds very expensive, but I'm sure we can find it. We'll share a cab.' 'But there's no evidence it's the way you want to go.' 'There's every evidence,' he said, 'as far as I'm concerned.'

She observed, having nothing of her own to look at, that the papers on his knee comprised the table of contents for some literary conspectus. 'One of the books you've written?' she asked. 'One of the ones I'm going to write,' he said. 'How come it already has an index and page numbers, if it isn't written yet?' 'We start with those,' he said, 'these days. Publishing is now a branch of futurology. I project, therefore

I am. Descartes before the horse, you might say.' 'Forgive me looking,' she said, 'but I'm not used to being without something to read, it's like being naked.' 'Allow me to lend you something to cover your nakedness, though I must say you wear it with a good deal of style.' 'Tell me,' she said, 'how often do you travel up to see your wife and children?' '*Ex*-wife and children. When I can. Once or twice a month.' 'I wonder if I've ever seen you before,' she said. 'Yes,' he said, 'I wonder.'

They stood side by side in the queue for taxis, decorously impatient. The cabs had to come down a narrow ramp and execute a hairpin turn at the bottom. People shouted 'oy!' as burdened travellers, or foreigners unfamiliar with local proprieties, sought to board prematurely. 'There's really no need,' she said, 'for you to take me to the hospital. The driver'll know where it is.' 'Why deny me the pleasure? I've nothing else to do before midday. I shan't assault you, I promise.' 'Oh, I'm not worried about that,' she said. As he opened the door of the ticking taxi, she put the return half of her ticket in the inside tuck of her purse and straightened her gloves.

While the cab was moving up the ramp to the street, he said: 'Listen, I swear to you I've never said anything like this to a stranger before, and I probably only could say it to a stranger, but I very much want to make love to you. Love.' 'Look,' she said, 'I honestly think it'd be better if I got out —' 'No, please. I mean it. You have extraordinary eyes: you must have Mediterranean blood somewhere — Egyptian possibly or Persian — and I find you enormously attractive. Something happened in that train, you know it did.' 'We were both out of breath at the same time,' she said, 'coming from different places, and going to different places.' 'Can't you see your cousin later in the day? I want to take you somewhere and undress you and caress you, very gently, very slowly, and really make it last. How can I persuade you that I'm really sincere?' 'I believe you're really sincere,' she said, 'but you can't persuade me.' 'Deny that it appeals to you, the idea. Deny that you're tempted. Not with those eyes, you can't. You've got too much pride to tell yourself a lie.' 'But not too little to tell you one,' she said. 'Two transient creatures on a transient earth,' he said. 'I'm a transient creature with a home and a husband and children and a sick, frightened cousin who's waiting for me,' she said. 'Two hours in a hotel,' he said, 'and we both have something to bank against oblivion. What on earth makes you say no?' 'Perhaps you making the decision mine,' she said, and then put up a gloved hand against his kiss. 'You said you wouldn't.' 'Promise me something, promise me that if we ever meet again like that, if it ever happens again, we won't talk, we won't say a word, but when we get to London, you'll come with me to a hotel and make love. It'll almost certainly not happen, but promise me that if it does ... ' 'Certainly not,' she said. 'That's a bargain then,' he said, and opened the door for her to get out. 'Where are we going now then, guv?' the driver said. He gave the address of a members-only library, his eye on the little red figure punched up on the clock, denoting extras. His late companion sat there with him still and he frowned to see the date against her name in the unwritten chapter of his future contents.

She did everything she had scheduled and even had time for a new hair-do, a present for her husband. She told him she never wanted to go to London again and embraced him breathlessly. But some three or four weeks later, she told him that it was maddening, but she simply had to go up to town. There were several things she wanted to do and some-one she had to see.

For Joannie

So far she has only been a model, *the* model: her face on every fashionable plate. The world leans towards her with its most amiable smile. Beauty could be some sort of handicap, everyone is so kind. Her pettiest achievement is coddled with applause; her prettiest hesitation prompts helping hands. Yet when she hears that the great director wants her in his next film, she is less complacent than incredulous: 'But I can't act,' she says.

Her agent twirls his *kir royal* between browned fingers and looks into those expensive eyes. 'Angel,' he says, 'modelling is acting. Maybe the most demanding kind of acting there is. No script, right? You don't do anything, you just are. And that's exactly what a movie star does: she just *is*. You've been acting all your sweet life, and now here's your chance to work with the king. This is your time, angel. The bells are ringing. Are you seriously not going to answer them?'

She sips her blackcurrant champagne, and puckers her short, never snub, nose. 'It's not just any old stand-there part, Jonathan. I have *lines*. Scads of them. Did you see the script?'

'Did I see it? I weighed it.' He presses the cool Scorpio from his necklet to the centre of his forehead and drops it against his Fiorucci chest. 'Angel, you're not a girl who has to winch her way to the top. I'm aiming to ease you down right there on the summit. Everest-time, sweetheart. Don't be afraid of it: the guy's a genius.'

'Everest and a genius and all at the same time! Did you ever hear of vertigo?'

24

'Let's not talk about old movies. Angel, you're the most beautiful woman in the world. Would you be five hundred an hour if you weren't? He'll be lucky to have you. And remember: they came to us. Nobody's snowing anybody. I never told them you studied with Strasberg. This is a director who could get an award-winning performance out of my aunt Sophie.'

'You mean the one that studied with Strasberg?'

'At least meet with him, angel. At least take the meeting. Your first picture and I'm going in there to talk about seven figures.'

'You won't get them,' she says.

'But I'm sure as hell going in there to talk about them. You're worth it, kid. Believe me, you're more than a pretty face.'

'So are you, Jonathan.'

'Well, I work out, don't I? Let me tell you something else: I'm talking to them about Joannie for the Countess. I wasn't going to tell you, but I am. I'm already actively into that.'

'Are you really?'

'No, not really. But I will be. I know she's on their wanted list because Howard Roth told me she was. You know Howie.'

'I know Joannie and she's a hell of an actress. With her along, it'd give me terrific reassurance.'

'You and I are sharing the same space on this one, angel. She'd be a plus in her own right for the picture and she'd be terrifically supportive for you personally.'

'Can we make it a condition of sale?'

'Sure we can,' Jonathan says, 'sure we can, unless it turns out we can't.'

The director lives at the beach. His wife thinks Beverly Hills is 'tacky'. They rarely come into town; they never go to the parties. He works at home. His house is equipped with its own cutting and projection rooms, but then so is everybody's. In addition, however, he has the very latest electronic gadgetry: he can scan a dozen different versions of a sequence within just a few minutes. He can entertain entertaining possibilities beyond the means, and the patience, of less technological men. He never hurries and he always worries. He looks for flaws even in perfection. He can be like some perverse alchemist, tireless in pursuit of a formula for turning gold into lead. All of his films are odd-balls and all of them have bounced clear the way to the top.

He says he will arrange a car to bring her out to Malibu. She dresses and dresses again, undresses and re-dresses, until she is satisfied. ('Joannie, promise me he'll really think I didn't have time to change.') When the car comes, he is driving it himself for chrissake, a guy like that! ('Joannie, are you *sure?*') It is a ranch-wagon, with defective trim and rusty gouges out of the side. When he first sees her coming, he pushes open the buckled door and leans over and greets her with his sallow face almost down on the passenger seat: 'Hey, kid, you want to be in the movies?' She gives a comic shrug, a young girl robbed of both composure and nervousness at one neat stroke. The back of the car is choked with electronic junk he introduces to her as his new chess opponent, Basil.

That night she tells Joannie what a terrific day they had. 'I was really impressed, I mean *really*. He has the whole movie in his head already, but at the same time he's flexible. Like *he* was asking *me* what I thought.'

'And what's she like?'

'She's a superb cook. We had these *blintzes*... Personally? Very secure. Strong. A wise woman. She's kind of small and dumpy, but *attractive*, you know. I'll tell you something you may not believe: we talked about you more than we did about me. He's truly thrilled about you playing the Countess. He's some admirer of Joannie Hanson, this guy, believe me. You're going to love him.'

'Don't wait for me,' Joannie says. 'You go right ahead.'

'Don't worry: he knows all about us. No hassle. Anyway, I told you: he has this wife.'

'One for you, one for me.'

'She doesn't only cook, by the way. She's also an astounding water-colourist. Gifted? God! You should see her things.'

'So you're going to do it, right?'

'All I have to do is stand there.'

His attentiveness does not slacken, even when the deals are finally inked. He stops by the house to take her personally to fittings and make-up sessions. When she wants Joannie along, he positively values her advice and experience. Pretty soon they are having family barbecues on the sanitised sand below the beach house with the kids from his first marriage. By the time shooting is due, the girls are in total agreement: he is something else. And what about those water-colours of hers?

When the limousine comes up the driveway past the mail-box to their stilted little house above Benedict Canyon at six o'clock on the first day of principal photography, she is almost surprised (and a little disappointed) not to see him at the wheel. He is on a high rostrum when they walk across the Spanish set, nodding their good mornings to the chippies who can always chisel and check out chicks at the same time. He looks down when they look up, but he is plotting a stand-in's position through his view-finder. The stand-in reads a yachting magazine in a two-foot wig and Bermuda shorts. A third-assistant comes up to Joannie with just a few changes for the scene they were going through in the car. They hope to be ready for the star right after lunch. Meanwhile would she like to check out her caravan while Miss Hanson goes to make-up? She finds a gift on the counter: a perfect little pot of rhinestone caviare. 'Don't eat it all at once,' the card says, signed 'the ogre'. ('The great thing about being regarded as an ogre,' he told them one day at the beach, 'is you don't get too many callers at the house. So occasionally you have to eat a kid. So?')

Joannie is almost unrecognisable when she next sees her. She has on the wig and the crinoline and her face is a beauty-spotted mask. She seems very calm. Only the pinch and flare of the powdered nostrils indicate how she is having to control herself.

They walk through a rehearsal. The Countess has to step from the cut-out of a carriage and walk across the patio of Don Juan's house to where Robert (two million dollars and ten per cent of the gross) is giving orders to his servant, referred to by the crew as 'scare-a-mouse'. The Countess has to argue with him for a rewritten moment and then pull out a pistol and fire it at Juan's breast. The rehearsal is complicated by a proposed swallow-dive from the camera on the big crane, a bitch of a shot for a first morning, which is why the director has scheduled it. ('My pool,' he once told them, 'only has a deep end.')

They reach the noon break without having even tried for a shot. The director stays on the set. He has not spoken to the actors. They eat in their costumes, over which a bumbling wardrobe lady arranges muslin bibs. Joannie can hardly move and never speaks.

After lunch, things are at last ready for a trial take. 'Action!' Joannie climbs from the cut-out barouche and walks flawlessly across the floor. The second camera pans as planned and is right there, on cue, as Juan, with a flick of gloved fingers, dusts gunpowder and spent dialogue from his doublet, while the Countess sinks to his uncreased knees. 'And cut.'

The director comes down from the rostrum in his stained denims and goes first to the cut-out and then slowly across the patio, making knight's moves, his sneakers avoiding the lines. He looks at Robert and then at Joannie. He might be seeing her for the first time in his life. 'Is that it?' he says.

'Did I do something wrong?'

'You're the actress,' he says.

'Jonathan!' The agent and his beautiful client are standing at the corner of the set, behind one of the brutes. 'Why is he *doing* this? Why is he trying to destroy Joannie?'

'Nobody's being destroyed, angel. This is the movies. Joannie can handle it.'

They do the scene sixteen more times. They never reach the next set-up at all that day. Joannie is totally exhausted when they finally get into the homing limousine. Even without her make-up, she looks different: distant and drained. Yet she resumes the next morning with no sign of apprehension. Can she be unaware of how she was humiliated? He *is* an ogre. 'Jonathan, why is he *doing* this? Is he going to treat me this way?'

'Angel, relax.'

Relax? By the time they line up her first shot, she has forgotten all the generous weeks of preparation, the homey huddles and hamburgers over the script, the video-taped improvisations, the electronic evenings with Basil. She has a long walk and then a short line, direct to camera. Can she ever do it? 'Action.' She does it. Has she said the six words in the right order? 'Cut.' He comes down from the camera car and walks up to her and stares at her for a long, unsmiling moment. Then he leans forward and kisses her on the lips. 'Ace,' he says. 'Next set-up.'

He drops her off at Benedict Canyon himself that night. She walks on up to the shaded sun-deck where Joannie, who has not been scheduled this week, is watching her arrival. 'I bet he was just giving me an easy ball,' she says over her chilled Chablis. 'What odds that shot isn't even in the final cut? He'll probably come down like the wolf on the fold pretty soon now.'

'And don't I know which fold?' Joannie says. 'You know he wants me off the picture, don't you?'

'Come on. He said to say hullo. He said specially. *Joannie*. Come back here.'

Jonathan has to give her the news when they are down in Mexico, shooting the bull-fight. There have been big little hold-ups over insurance, because Bobby insists on doing all his veronicas himself and even a shaved horn can make a big hole in two million dollars, and the gross. 'Angel, it's really very simple. It's nobody's fault but we're six weeks behind already and I have Joannie contracted for a play she really wants to do in New York, goes into rehearsal in a month and a half. They were going to shoot her scenes finishing last week and instead...'

'Did he plan this, Jonathan? If he planned this...'

'Who plans this kind of a thing?'

'Because I told you before: Joannie goes, I go.'

'Suppose you talk to Joannie about this. Because she has a lot of respect for you, angel, and you quit now, how much of it is going to be left? Joannie is a disciplined professional. You talk to her about it.'

'He postponed shooting on her three times to my knowledge. He planned this.'

'Angel, I give you my word of honour...'

'I never heard of a Scorpio with one of those before,' she says. 'Or two of *them*, if it comes to that.'

'*Angel.*'

Joannie says of course she has to stay. They will be together again when the picture's in the can. It is too true that she has this play to do. She is not in the least resentful and she absolutely does not feel betrayed or let down. 'Baby, you have this week's greatest director in the world in love with you, you're giving a performance, he has people waiting in line to see the rushes, so for my sake, never mind yours, don't blow it, O.K.? We may need the bread.'

'In love with me? I'll give him in love with me.'

'You do that. For Joannie, O.K.?'

Joannie flies out, alone, with flowers. Soon there comes an invitation to have dinner with the great man in the penthouse.

His wife has a one-woman show opening in San Francisco, otherwise she would have loved to be there. He gives her a *tequila* and speaks sincerely about Joannie. 'Two into one just wouldn't go,' he says, squatting on a mirror-studded cushion by her feet and toying with the golden chain that graces her ankle. 'She was giving a very professional performance, she really was.' He raises tired, almost pleading eyes to hers and is amazed by the sudden, swallow-diving kiss, full on his salty lips. 'Oh,' he says, 'I don't remember that in the script.'

'You haven't seen the changes then, have you?'

'I loved you when I only knew you in two dimensions,' he says. 'And now... I'm eighteen again.'

'Listen, I'll play the eighteen-year-olds around here, O.K.?' she says. 'I knew we were going places the minute I saw that ratty-looking car of yours. Just my style!'

'I had those panels beaten in specially for you, didn't I?'

'Yes? And how about Joannie? You had her beaten in too, didn't you?'

'You're wrong there.'

'All's fair, right?'

'That's unfair. I recognise Joannie's quality. I also recognise you and she... and I can understand that. Now it's time to graduate. Baby's gotta walk! After all, you said you wanted to play eighteen.'

'Be nice to me,' she says. 'Because I'm crossing the line here, you know that, don't you? This is strictly a first for me, no kidding.'

He is nice. He is gentle and confident and, in tactfully due course, as nice as he can be. She moans and she says 'Oh' and '*Oh*' and she does things she has never done before as if she has already done them all. At last he judges the moment right for the right moment: at the climactic brink, sure that she is tumbling with him, he flings himself, with a last spurt, irrevocably over. 'I love you,' he says. 'I love you. Oh, how I love you!'

She is looking down at him and there is unmelted ice in those by-the-hour eyes. '*Well*,' she says, 'is that it?'

That Was Tory

'Oh God,' Clive said, 'what did she want?'

'Not what she's got,' Gigi said, 'that much is evident. Dunk's done a bunk.'

'I don't think I'm with you,' Clive said.

'Duncan, your old and trusted friend, has walked out.'

'*Duncan* has? I can't believe it. When?'

'Last weekend apparently. After Fiona's Parents' Day. The poor lady sounds as though she's been in tears ever since. Not that I blame her. I'm sure I shall be in precisely the same condition the day you decide that the children are now quite old enough—'

'The children are quite old enough now,' Clive said, 'but I'm not. If anyone's liable to walk out, it certainly isn't me. As past events have proved, though we won't bother about that one now. Anyway, I hate walking. Funny, I always thought if either of them went, it'd be her. You still haven't said what she wanted.'

'Just a fresh shoulder to cry on, I think, poor girl.'

'She's hardly a girl at this point, is she? She must be a good forty.'

'There's no such thing,' Gigi said, 'as a good forty.'

'You look better than ever,' Clive said, 'and what's more you know it. You could have a perfectly good life without me. What about that Arab last week? He was practically offering you gold bathroom taps for openers. Incidentally, this quiche is absolutely ace. You've got the pastry bang right this time. And the Meursault goes very well with it. Pretty impressive, don't you agree, we can still do a bottle of this quality at under three-fifty? How the hell's Duncan going to manage without her?'

'With a little help from his friend, one assumes.'

'Oh, he's got one of those, has he?'

'It's always the woman who gets whacked in the end, isn't it?'

'She wasn't very clever with him, was she, when you come to think about it?'

'Just because you never liked her.'

'I never showed I didn't.'

'No,' she said, 'and it showed.'

'Apart from that very first time when I lashed out and she burst into tears on me. I never saw a grown woman crying until that moment. I'd assumed she was rock-hard Knightsbridge through and through. Must be fifteen years ago now. More. Silly argument about nothing, but even you had to admit I was right.'

'Everybody did,' Gigi said. 'What she really wants is a job.'

'Only she can't do anything, I know. What about getting her to answer the phone to your sheiks and people?'

'We have precisely one sheik; the office is two by two; and what would Crispin say?'

'I daresay he wouldn't find that noble bosom much of a turn-on, dear Crispin.'

'Is it that noble?'

'She wasn't a bad-looking girl *à l'époque*. Quite attractive, if only she hadn't had a touch of the debs about her.'

'I always thought that was the attraction. She can type a bit, she said, and she's got some French. She was finished in Switzerland, you may remember.'

'Positively château-bottled, I know, but what am I supposed to do with her?'

'She doesn't mind what she does.'

'People always say they'll do anything, but they always

mean anything except what you want them to do. She can't exactly hump crates of Xmas booze about the place, can she? It's really up to Duncan to find her something. God knows, the Ministry of Transport's big enough for two these days. Frankly, it's the least he can do.'

'But more than he's prepared to.'

'She would do him such a bloody great favour all the time.'

'For which he had more than good reason to be grateful. At least at the beginning. You may remember his feet.'

'She did cope with his feet.'

'She also worked her way up. She even got him to wear shirts that weren't a size too small. *And* she eliminated the heavy breathing.'

'Suffocation does that,' Clive said. 'Unfortunately it eliminates breathing of all kinds, which is presumably why he done what he done finally.'

'He's a shit, after all those years she propped him up. They always seemed happy enough.'

'We rather guessed there was something wrong, didn't we, that last time we went there? It was in the depths of winter and they gave us prawn salad, followed by tinned rhubarb which did absolutely horrible things to a rather nice bottle I'd brought.'

'I still think it was the wrong night,' Gigi said. 'No one else turned up, which was rather ominous, and Duncan had a suspiciously blank look on his face when he opened the front door. Not that he wasn't capable of looking blank on the right night too, of course, when he was in one of his moods. When one thinks about it, could anyone have been more patient than she was?'

'Which makes it all the more surprising he didn't check out years ago. Imagine what all that Knightsbridge patience must have been like in bed.'

'One never knows what people get up to in bed. I don't honestly think you can draw any inferences.'

'Then that's because you don't think honestly.'

'Would you like the rest of the quiche, my darling? And if so, in which eye?'

'She did him a lot of good on the surface and underneath she humiliated him. Like you with me.'

'Oh sure.'

'She'll find someone. Whom do we know that's lonely?'

'There's always Cecil.'

'Apart from Cecil.'

'What about Tony Lovecraft up in Norwich?'

'He's up in Norwich, though, isn't he? I expect she's got bags of friends. If I hear of anything in the job department, I'll obviously give her a ring, but she has rather left it a bit, and I'm up to my bloody eyes, what with the spring catalogue *and* Christmas.'

'You might be able to do with some help in that case.'

'The trouble is, my darling, some help never helps.'

'I'll ask Crispin,' Gigi said, 'but I can't see him being keen.'

Gigi and her partner, Crispin Trenchard, ran their interior decorating business with hermetic efficiency. After the first consultations, not even the client was admitted to the premises on which they were working until the place was ready for occupation. Clive was invited the night before, to enjoy a test pilot's brief *droit de seigneur*, after which Gigi and Crispin accepted his compliments, allowed him to insert six of the best bottles shipped by Redman and Slater into the kitchen bin and delivered the key (and the account) to the client.

A few days after the sorry news about Tory Jameson, the telephone rang in Clive's office and the trunk-calling voice of a country solicitor ('Oh, Ivor McCauseland here from Ipswich, Mr Redman') was afraid to say that an old customer of the firm had died and that the executors would be immensely obliged if Clive could dispose of the rather important cellar for them, in the usual way. Since the law required the contents to be sold at auction, it meant cataloguing, didn't it, and transport? Clive said, 'Yes, of course,' and put the telephone down and said, 'Damn.' He then called Tory and asked her to have lunch with him.

'It's probably rather a miserable job and damnably chilly too, if I know anything about country house cellars, but there it is: honour says it needs doing and I don't suppose you'd find it very difficult.'

'I don't mind what I do,' she said, 'and it sounds fascinating.'

'No, it doesn't, Tory, and it certainly won't be, but the executors'll pay you a few bob and it might take your mind off your troubles, or give you a surreptitious chance to drown them, assuming they still exist. Take a corkscrew, whatever you do!'

She was wearing a floppy hat and a pink suit. Her shoes were rather pretty: pale toffee, with a narrow strap round the ankle and over the instep into a diminutive gold buckle. 'You are kind, Clive,' she said.

'Well, there we are then,' he said. 'The best thing is to go down to Ipswich on Monday – they'll put you up in a hotel – and that way you'll have the best part of two days, which should be ample. Old McCauseland swears most of the bins are labelled, but you'll probably end up by having to scrape a certain amount of rat shit away to locate the Taylors'. I'll buzz down Tuesday p.m. and tidy up the odds and ends with you, O.K.?'

'You are kind, Clive, really. How's Gigi?'

'Oh deep in her usual secrets. She and Crispin are tarting up a penthouse for some chic sheik. Have you met Crispin?'

'It's a long time since I saw either of you,' she said.

'Well, we've been through the standard mid-life crises, but things aren't too bad. Gigi's making a terrific success of the business. Crispin's turned out to be a godsend. What's the right term for an affair between a married woman and a homosexual, do you know? *Une affaire blanche*, perhaps.'

'Delicious smoked trout!' she said. 'This is the first time I've felt hungry since it happened. I don't think I'd've minded so much if he hadn't shown me her photograph.'

'Not very tactful of him.'

'She's so plain,' Victoria said. 'That's what hurt.'

'How's Fiona taking it?'

'She's glued to her horse. Yoiks tally-ho and I haven't seen her since, honestly.'

'I always took you to have been rather horsey, were you?'

'I never got further than rabbits.'

'I always thought you had the thighs for the job. Horses, I mean.'

'This is really an awfully nice place.'

'Yes, Michael doesn't run a bad kitchen, does he? His portions aren't getting any bigger, though, I notice. One favourable mention in the glossies and you can kiss the second vegetable goodbye. All he needs is a rosette in the Michelin and he'll stop giving salad either. Oh for God's sake, wear some trousers when you go down to Ipswich or you'll freeze to death. You didn't have an affair with Dickie Bannerman at one point, did you?'

'I never had an affair with anyone, Clive.'

'Sorry; I didn't mean to pry. Well, that's not quite true. It's rather strange this kind of thing, isn't it? Suddenly you aren't the same person; and at the same time it's perfectly evident that you are. Do you remember when I made you cry?'

'You never made me cry. You're thinking of somebody else.'

'Come on, Tory. It was virtually the first time we met. Dunk brought you round to the flat. We were living in that mansion block opposite South Ken. You slept in the sitting room and we all had breakfast the next morning and we were drinking our tea and burning the toast and you and I had this terrific flare up and it ended with you bursting into tears. We went for each other like mad. Surely you remember? It was basically political.'

'I remember the flat,' she said, 'and how nervous I was.'

'You looked as cool as Harrods. That's why I was so

embarrassed. It's coloured my whole attitude to you ever since.'

'You've always been very sweet.'

'That's what I mean.'

'Will you thank Gigi for me, when you see her?'

'She was really sorry for you the other day. So sorry she gave me quite a *mauvais quart d'heure* about the iniquity of the male sex. How you hate us really, all of you, don't you?'

'I never hated anybody,' she said. 'That was what was so ghastly with old Dunkie: the things he dredged up out of the past. Things I'd begged him to talk about and he never would. Suddenly out they came. How I'd failed to do this or let him do that—and all the time I'd really thought he quite liked me—'

'I know,' Clive said, miming more coffee for the waiter.

'You and Gigi can talk. We never could. It was all—iced over—like a cake. I kept a piece of my wedding cake for years and then one day I opened the little box—a sort of baby silver coffin it was—to show Fiona, because she was at the tea-party stage, and the whole thing was mouldy—green dust, horrible! He seems to have thought I was a monster, Clive. Am I?'

'I used to think you were a bit stuck up. I certainly don't think you're a monster.'

'I really thought everything was fine. Stuck up? I always considered myself very easily satisfied. I never wanted much.'

'Or you wouldn't have married Duncan,' Clive said, 'would you?'

'I had an idea, when I was a little girl, that if you were enough like other people nothing bad ever happened to you. Even death. And now this has. I don't know: perhaps I deserve it.' She stirred her new coffee. 'I'd love to see Gigi some time.'

'I'm sure she'd love to see you,' he said.

The Parsonage was a double-gabled pink farmhouse, in the Suffolk style, with a bell on an iron hoop outside the front door. He arrived towards the end of a yellowish afternoon, the sky stacked with fuming clouds which seemed to carry lurid reflections of some invisible conflagration. The road was wet with a storm he had not experienced.

He jangled the bell, but no one answered, so he pushed open the door and went into the flagged hallway. 'Victoria?' Pictures had already been stripped from the rosy walls. The hall was narrowed by a dressing table and a dismantled bedstead which the men had evidently abandoned until the next day. An elephant's foot full of canes and walking sticks stood under the stairs. 'Victoria?' The house was cold. Through the hall window he could see fresh rain falling into the gravel; it sounded like boiling fat. 'Anyone here?' The deserted house had the unsettling stillness of a corpse.

Clive ambled into the drawing room. Beside the chimney-piece, a collection of German bandsmen stood tall in a glass barrack. In the bookshelves, slumped volumes, their more valuable neighbours already gone to auction, had lost their dignity. An urge to steal something began to beat in Clive like a pulse. He sighed and made loud footsteps across the hall and into the gunroom, in search of the kitchen. 'Victoria?'

There was china in crates on the laundry table in the scullery. Clive edged a blue-hooped saucer to the end of the table and allowed it to crash onto the hard floor. On the mantelpiece, like a last invitation, stood a box of matches. Through a rounded doorway, the kitchen proper displayed a startling modernity. Had some plausible salesman sold the old man all the latest pine and formica or had his cook blackmailed it out of him?

A door was ajar on the far side of the kitchen. A dull light, the shade of marmalade, shone from below. Clive went down the noisy steps. Victoria was sitting on a stack of crates in the middle of the cellar. Her face was veiled with cobwebs. She was wearing a tweed suit. 'Oh Clive,' she said.

'You couldn't manage it,' he said.

'I've been at it for two solid days.'

'Have you?' he said. 'Then what's the problem?'

'I've done all this side,' she said, 'but over here it doesn't make any sort of sense at all. Some of the bottles haven't even got labels. He just bunged things wherever he felt like it.'

'Disobliging fellow,' Clive said. 'What about these? They seem fairly simple to deal with.'

'I've done most of those,' she said. 'It's these.'

'Well, come on, cheer up, let's get on with it. Here I am. Why aren't you wearing trousers?'

'I don't like trousers,' she said.

'I told you to wear trousers. How can you expect to work in that? This isn't a bloody point-to-point, you know.'

'I'm perfectly happy in this, don't worry.'

'No wonder you're all hot and bothered. I'll tell you what we'll do, we'll work through everything that's in half dozens or more and we'll liberate the rest.'

'Liberate? What's liberate?'

'Liberate. What's the matter with you? We'll drink the bloody stuff. Help ourselves. Oh for goodness' sake, Victoria—'

'I'll be all right in a minute. I was just so afraid you'd be angry.'

'I am bloody angry. Now come on, you've got work to do. If you'd worn trousers, you wouldn't have got yourself into such a state. Take that bloody skirt off and we'll get to work.'

'I'm all right now.'

'Take it off when I tell you. Why can't you do as you're told? No wonder Dunk pissed off.'

She took cobweb from her hair and wiped it onto the un-sanded wood of the wine-rack in the recess behind her. The breath sounded in her nostrils as she unzipped her skirt and stepped out of it. She was wearing a pink slip. 'All right?'

'Now let's get this done,' Clive said.

They worked without speaking. When one section was cleared and catalogued, he indicated the next. He might have been training an animal. The bare light was glossy on her pink slip as she bent and straightened. Sweat scalded her eyes.

By the time they had finished, they had been in the cellar

for close on five hours. As the last lot was tabulated (eight bottles of Château la Tour du Pin, 1937), she stood panting in front of him. 'I'm so sorry it wasn't all done before you got here,' she said. 'I did mean it to be.'

'I don't mind about that,' he said, 'but I specifically told you to wear trousers. Why didn't you? I'm talking to you. I didn't tell you to put your skirt on again, did I? Why are you?'

'Clive, don't be silly. We've finished.'

'I haven't,' he said. 'Take it off again. Take everything off.'

'Clive, really, it's late.'

'But not too late.'

'Gigi'll be waiting,' she said.

'Gigi!' he said. 'Take your bloody clothes off when I tell you. If you don't do as I say, you'll be sorry.' He picked up a bottle and broke its neck against the brickwork. Victoria started to unbutton her jacket. When she was naked, he looked at her in the light of the dulling bulb and then he sloshed the sharp wine over her breasts and shoulders from the jagged neck of the bottle. It ran down her rumpled stomach and bloodied her groin. She stood at last in wet sandals. 'There,' he said, 'how do you like that?'

'I don't mind,' she said. 'I don't mind if you kill me, if that's what you want.'

He slapped her breast. It was loud with the wine and shook, glistening. 'All I consciously intended,' he said, 'was to do you a good turn, you silly cow.'

'I know,' she said. She reached to touch him. In the stale heat, fumes from the wine came from her body. 'Is there something you want me to do?' she said. 'I will.'

'Why is everything so terrible, Victoria?' he said, at last. 'We have the chance to lead pleasant, civilised lives and everything is absolutely terrible. Why?'

'Oh God,' she said, 'I don't know,' and sighed and reached for her slip and began to wipe her feet.

Forgetting It

They returned to the island while the spring flowers were still moist. (Summer would see them dry.) The cottage was a ruin; the weeds on the breached roof a calendar of neglect. A long-lashed donkey looked out from where the door had been, eyes spectacular with flies. 'No one lives here any more,' she said.

'Oh,' he said, 'it could probably be cleaned out in no time.'

'No,' she decided.

They walked back along the rocky path towards the harbour. The unmortared walls prevented them going side by side. Two men were painting the stained concrete of the shuttered hotel with round brushes fixed to broom-handles. The painters had made paper caps of yesterday's headlines.

They sat at the café under the arcade on the quayside. A sign on the cracked window said: 'We catch, we cook, we serve.' They looked out at the white church (named for peace) with its twin racks of silent bells, glistening on a shelf above the shuffling water. One could sense coming heat; it was held off by a last screen of spring mist. He moved his chair, as if preliminary to broaching a subject which lay, like that heat, just the far side of declaration. Did he hope that she would start? He strained for a cue, eyes loaded with pleading reproach. 'You're just as beautiful as ever,' he said. Was this the unpopular subject?

He sighed and raised his cup. The boiling coffee bit his tongue. He swallowed pain like a pill. 'Drink some water,' she said.

He inspected her hand, quite as if it had been left there on the table and he wanted to see whose it was. While he looked at it, she was looking at him. 'You think we shouldn't have come,' he said. 'You think we've done the wrong thing.'

'Do I?' she said. 'I don't think I do.'

The calf of one leg was fattened by the knee it rested on. Its whiteness dismayed him; he might have brought an invalid with him. He wanted her strong, so that he need no longer be, so that he might cry out, might be more like her. But first she had to be like herself and this she refused. She resembled that sullen heat couched behind the spring mist, ardent with denial.

'We can always catch the next steamer,' he said, 'if this was a bad idea. There are other islands, lots of them. Shall we go or shall we stay?'

'I don't mind,' she said.

He said her name several times.

There was no steamer for another four days; they might as well see if there was a house they liked. Summer residents left their keys with a Roumanian caretaker in the village; there was quite a choice. Things had changed since the year they rented the cottage from a peasant who had never seen a typewriter. (Niko was rich now, from the summer tourists, and spent winters in the capital; his daughter was learning to be a stenographer.) They chose a modern place, a whitewashed tower with a flagged terrace from which the owner, in a blazer, could judge the seamanship of summer yachtsmen as they made anchor below the church.

He smiled, as they agreed the inventory, to see the luxuries they had come to do without. But how could one complain at the wide Dunlopillo mattress? It was better than Niko's straw. (Once, going into the cottage's tree-beamed bedroom, she had yelped at a pyjama-striped stranger humped in their narrow bed. He called her crow for a while, because she had been scared, his fair wife.) 'There we are then,' he said, as the gas popped and glimmered blue, 'everything seems to work.'

Each day he took, as he had taken, a fresh lease of patience. He was on a kind of emotional diet; he lived slim. Rage whispered in him, wary infidel in a cathedral. He could not blame her, and blamed her for it. And she? Dutiful regularity was promptly installed; meals appeared, tasty as ever, but his compliments did not warm her. She ate a standard portion, playing the patient taster for his sake. (The seconds were all for him.) Her consideration denied him mourning.

They slept apart on the comfortable mattress, under the gathered mosquito net they had no need to use.

On the third day, the sun lanced the caul of mist. Shadows sprang on the hillsides, detail stippling the rocks. The village houses stood forward, black-eyed. They walked up, past bolted cafés stencilled with vacant summer invitations and smiled at the flat-footed peasants, if not at each other. The donkeys' hooves scuttered on the shallow steps and the peasants grabbed their tails.

The beach beyond the village was a hooped moon of sand, eaten into eclipse by the working sea. Knobs of pumice bobbed grey against the winter jetsam. They sat in the new sun and he spread oil onto her whiteness. She would wear her swimsuit, despite the solitude. Did she not know that the beach was notorious, in the season, for its nudity? And now who could see them? 'I'm all right,' she said.

He could not be naked with her covered. He sat in his jeans, head forward over dry sand he heaped and heaped between his knees. He got up at last and walked down to the sea, showing a passing interest in shells. The water scalded his foot, it was so cold. He undid his belt and finally stood naked at the hem of the water and looked back at her. She had turned on her face, hands latched under her forehead, white soles exposed. He punched his shins into the water, left, right, left, and thrust himself down into the icy punishment.

When he came back, she turned on one elbow and rumpled

her forehead, freckled with sand. He bent and kissed dry lips. 'How was it?' she said.

'Cold. But very beautiful.'

She stretched her neck.

'Or did you mean the water?' he said. He crouched to put his mouth to her shoulder and pressed it there, like a brand. 'There are lots of fishes,' he said, at last. 'You'd think you could catch them with your hand, as many as you wanted, but of course you can't. Are we ever going to be able to talk?'

She was busy doing little things, flicking sand from her body, seeing what the time was. 'Of course,' she said, 'whenever you want to. What shall we talk about?'

'It wasn't either of our faults,' he said, 'was it? Was it my fault?'

'Of course not.'

'Well, I certainly don't think it was yours.'

'That's probably enough for one day,' she said. 'Sun, I mean.'

He stood up, dizzy, robbed of blood. The mountain in front of him was capped by a nipple of white, where an old monastery caught the sun. A green valley ran back from the beach and a peasant nudged his donkey between flower-pink bushes, coming at once towards them and away, threading a secret eye through the line of the already dry river. He had a little boy up behind him, whose brown legs drummed the animal's flank, feet flashing. The child waved and shouted something, greeting or abuse.

'It's not too late,' he said. 'Why is it too late?'

He touched her that night across the cool bed. She rolled towards him, but made no warmer move. She dared him, his wife, and he could not bring himself to her. Her meekness maimed him. He sat forward, bowed between his legs, and shook his head. When at last he looked over at her, she was asleep, legs apart, head averse. He got out of the bed and went on to the terrace. There was a light under the arcade; the café owner's wife was working at a fish with a knife. The ship's hooter fetched him round and he saw the cut of its bows in the oily water. Were there not other islands and other women?

They brought the American up to the house the next morning, the caretaker and a toothless, mocking man in a flat cap, carrying a whittled stick like an unhorsed jockey, a flannel vest buttoned to his creased throat. The stranger was not too tall and pale and shy. The three foreigners were being put together, all of them seemed to realise, as a kind of jest: they were of a class. When at last the caretaker and the mocking man went away, the three of them had to start again, as if they had not yet spoken at all.

'I'm real sorry busting in on you. They insisted – '

'It's always the same, don't worry about it. They can't believe one doesn't want company. And they tend to think that everyone who isn't one of them is, well, one of us, you might say.'

'Sure seems that way. Listen, I don't want to take up any more of your time. Thing is, I was here before and I wanted to see what it was like when nobody was around.'

'Nobody ever is.'

'Right,' the stranger said. 'My name's Russell, by the way, Russell Miller, if that's of any importance. To me it's like a tag. Are you a writer?'

'Our name's Moxon,' Charles said. 'I'm Charles and this is Kat. Katharine. No, I'm not a writer, I'm an actor. Why? So is Kat.'

'An actress,' Kat said. 'Or was.'

'Kat,' Russell said. 'That's nice. I figured being here on your own like this... I'm a writer. At least I'm a poet. I guess it isn't quite the same thing.'

'Do you want some coffee?' Kat said.

'I came here to be alone, you know,' Russell said. 'I certainly don't want to intrude on you people.'

'You're welcome,' Charles said. 'Miller eh? No relation of Henry, I suppose?'

'Well, I've heard of him, of course, but we're not related. There are a hell of a lot of Millers in the world.'

'And Henrys,' Kat said, from inside.

'I was thinking of that time he met an old enemy of his on some railway platform in Poland, I don't know if you ever read that bit, and they fell into each other's arms, they were so happy to see someone they knew and spoke their language. What was an old enmity at a time like that?'

'Only we're not enemies,' Russell said. 'Do you work in the movies at all? I might have seen your face.'

'I work mainly on the stage, and in television, London mostly.' He might have been auditioning, Charles, his voice catching American rhythms. 'Were you ever in London yet?'

'My wife died last Christmas,' Russell Miller said. 'We were planning to go.'

He wore cut-off jeans and a yellow T-shirt. His arms and legs were covered with blond hairs. He carried a nylon backpack. There was a curious polish on his high cheekbones, like rubbed marble. He had offered them smiles when he was introducing himself, but now as he drank Kat's coffee, his face fell into deeper lines. She stood over him with milk in a punctured can. Charles said: 'I'll have a little more of that, darling, if I may.'

'You're a poet,' Kat said. 'What sort of poetry?'

'I have some with me as a matter of fact.'

'You make a living by writing poetry?'

'I'm a motor mechanic,' Russell said. 'I work in a body-shop.'

'A motor mechanic, are you really?' Charles said.

'No, really, I'm a poet. I pretend to be a motor mechanic.'

Kat said, 'Do you want to have lunch with us?'

'Do you think poems should be read or spoken?' Charles said.

'If they're spoken right, they should be spoken, I guess. But I'm not too good at reading my own work. I guess I lack the confidence. And...'

'What?' Kat said.

'My wife died last Christmas,' Russell Miller said. 'And I write a lot about her.'

'That's terrible,' Charles said.

'Yes,' Russell said. 'She was very beautiful.' He showed them pictures of a rather plain girl. 'So I don't find it very easy right now.'

'Beautiful,' Charles said. 'You have children?'

'No,' the boy said. 'We never did. That's somebody else's there in the picture. My sister's.'

'Are you staying long?' Charles said.

'What – ?' Kat had begun to speak at the same time.

'I'm sorry,' Charles said. 'Darling...'

'I just wondered what your wife's name was.'

'Miriam,' the poet said. 'Her name was Miriam. I guess I'll stay a month maybe. I want to see if I can work. We came here, you see. Last summer. We had a great time. Were you ever here in the summer? It's great. Great music, great people; we met some amazing people. Now... I want to see if I can get something together for Miriam, if you know what I mean. You see, I stayed here and she went to Athens, to see the doctor. And that's when... I hope I won't be in your space or anything.'

'Don't worry about us,' Charles said. 'We don't have any exclusive rights.'

'Leave us some of your poems,' Kat said. 'If you feel like it.'

'Be happy to, ma'am,' Russell Miller said. 'I guess I'll go sleep down on the beach. I left my bedroll over at Flora's place. I don't imagine anyone will object, will they?'

'I can't imagine it,' Charles said.

'Only Miriam and I slept on the beach before and the police came down and there was kind of a heavy scene out there for a while. I heard they killed a guy here last summer, an Australian, got drunk, they beat his head in. Well, see you later. Thanks for the coffee, ma'am.'

Charles read the poems and passed them to his wife. She read others and passed them to him. 'He's not much of a poet,' Kat said, 'is he?' He laughed when she said that and shook his head. 'These are terrible, aren't they?' Kat said. 'They're embarrassing.'

'He'd better be one hell of a mechanic,' Charles said.

She went abruptly into the house (as if he had disagreed with her) and he could see her combing her hair. She had caught the sun; her legs gleamed under the denim skirt. It hung unevenly as she worked her raised arm. She had a body again.

'Let's have another one, Kat,' he said. 'Please.'

She took the poems with her when she went to the shops the next morning. He offered to go with her but he was sketching, wasn't he? He had brought a block with him, but this was the first time that he had opened it. He had a scalpel and some charcoal pencils and he sat on the wall of the terrace sharpening them. They broke easily; one had to be subtle. He watched her walk along the quay and over the little bridge towards the harbour beach. Russell was standing in the water up to his knees, combing his long fair hair. Charles felt the flesh quicken in his jeans as his wife went towards the boy. He put the scalpel and the charcoal pencil on the wall of the terrace and shaped his face with his hands.

She stood at the water's edge. The boy turned towards her but did not come out of the yellow water. They talked like that. The two painters, in their newsprint caps, were at the near end of the beach, on tiptoe with their broom-handles under the eaves of the whitening hotel. A boy rode past them on a donkey, jabbing a cruel little stick into its rump.

'Oh Charles,' she said later, 'it's so awful. I wish I wasn't me.'

'And I wish you were,' he said. 'Why didn't he come to supper?'

'He went up to the village,' she said.

'You had a long talk,' he said, 'didn't you?'

'He's very young,' she said.

'Come to bed,' Charles said. 'Blast you.'

They had been together too long for him not to know when she was resisting him, even when she was not. If they had not been married, whatever that meant, he might have won her. But since she was his, he could not take her. Some silly donkey called out its longing in the night.

'What did he have to say for himself? You haven't really said.'

'She was killed in an accident,' Kat said. 'She was twenty years old. She was pregnant, five months.'

'So that's why they were coming to London,' Charles said. 'Did you tell him?'

'He didn't ask,' she said. 'He gave me some more of his poems. He's very prolific.'

'If you hate me,' Charles said, 'hate me. But hate me in the open. Where we can make something of it. Hate me to some purpose, do you think you could? Hate me or leave me, or both. You're killing me with this; you're making me into what you always said I was, and I wasn't, something without any qualities of my own, something that can only – what? – reflect, isn't that what you said?'

She took her basket the next morning and went shopping, hair in a kerchief; the wind was coming. When she got back, she made lunch of tuna fish and pasta. He watched her fret the black pepper between her fingers before she brought the dish to the table.

'You've come to life,' he said. 'Did you see our friend?'

'Have I? Yes, I did, as a matter of fact.'

'Has he written you another poem?'

'He didn't see me,' she said. 'He was taking the sun.' She tilted her own head at an angle to the heat and closed her eyes, the actress again. When she opened them, she was smiling, and so was he, but not at the same thing; that was why they were smiling. 'Sitting against the hotel.'

'I'll bet he did see you,' Charles said.

They walked up to the post office after the shadows had begun to lengthen. There might be a telegram; one never knew when there would be work. There was nothing for them. ('There wouldn't be anything for me,' Kat said.) Some impulse, after her remark, made him say, 'Anything for Miller?'

The old postman looked over the tops of his spectacles, the foreign bundle still in his hand. There were letters which had never been collected and sounded as brittle as old blue leaves. He sorted through them and swivelled an envelope towards them: Russell Miller.

'We'd better tell him,' Charles said.

'I know him,' Kat said. 'I'll take it down to him.'

She turned the letter over. There was a panel for the sender's address. It came from Miriam Rapke, in Athens. It was dated the previous August.

'I don't think we should wish that on him,' Charles said.

'You give him?' the postman said.

'I give him,' Kat said.

'Kat,' Charles said, when they were outside, 'you can't give him that letter. You have no business – '

'I never said I was going to give it to him,' she said. 'And no, I have no business.'

'You said it a minute ago.'

'Oh to him,' she said.

'I think you should take it back in there,' he said. 'I really do.'

'Oh do you really?' she said.

'You can't give it to him, you can't not give it to him. You're forked, Kat.'

'We're all forked,' she said.

'This is immoral, Kat, it really is.'

'*Immoral*?' she said. 'You ass. You royal ass, you really are.'

'And cruel. What're you going to do with that letter, Kat? I think you should give it to me.'

'Is it addressed to you? What does it have to do with you?'

'You're asking me to be an accomplice,' he said. 'You're involving us both in – in something...'

'Immoral?' She arched her back, hair tawny in the reddening light. 'Cruel? Well?'

'Kat, give me that letter, will you please?'

'Go in and tell him you disassociate yourself from all responsibility, why don't you? Have me arrested! They can beat me up. One old letter, what does he care?'

'I want to know what you propose to do with the damned thing.'

'I know you do,' she said.

The letter lay on the table while they had their supper. He pushed his plate away. 'You'd better go take it to him,' he said. 'You've started this, you'd better go through with it.'

'You've caught the sun,' she said. 'Your face is all red. Have you got a temperature? You look red-hot.'

She seemed to him to be almost plump, her darkening skin packed with flesh, not fat, but alive and powerful.

'Give me the letter,' he said, 'and I'll go and give it to him.'

'Don't be ridiculous,' she said.

'Ridiculous?' he said. '*Ridiculous?*'

'Of course,' she said. 'Why would he want you to give it to him?'

'It's his letter, goddammit,' he said. 'It's his and I'd be giving it to him.'

'Goddammit!' she said. 'Must you do imitations?'

'Kat, I want that letter. Do I have to take it from you?'

'Yes,' she said.

'I'm not afraid of you,' he said.

'I don't care what you are,' she said, the letter against her breast.

'Giving him that letter would be an act of cruelty I wouldn't normally believe you capable of.'

'You don't know what I'm capable of,' she said.

'Hurt me,' he said, 'if you're going to hurt anyone. If you're going to hurt anyone, hurt me.'

She walked out of the house and he stared after her; she might have quit the stage before her cue. By the time he had accepted that she was not coming back, she was already on the way to the harbour. She was gone into the purple of the evening. He could have caught her but he stayed there on the terrace. There was some element in her which was beyond him and always had been and that difference had now coloured her completely, as night had purpled the island. He went into the house and found the packet of new poems which Russell had offered in exchange for the ones she returned. He took the hot lamp from the table and carried it onto the terrace and from there he acted the poet's lines into the darkness. He shouted their faults.

She went along the beach to where the bedroll showed darker than the darkness. As she walked she unbuttoned the many-buttoned cardigan she had put on. Standing above him, she shivered; her body burned with the cold, like a glow-worm. She bent down, the shine of her flesh folding a shadow in its centre like a child, and crinkled the letter. He swam up out of his dream towards her. He was hot with it. 'Miriam?' he said. 'Miriam?'

'Yes,' she said, 'yes, my darling; yes, my baby.'

From over the bay the shouting ceased. There came now only the sound of a donkey bellowing into the night.

Welcome Aboard

'We finally did it,' Gabe said, as they turned left into First Class, 'we finally got someplace ahead of time. We finally didn't have to rush. This represents some kind of a breakthrough and I should like to congratulate us.'

'Hullo, sir, madam, did you enjoy your holiday?'

'How do you like that? If it isn't the smiling Mr Mountain!'

'Hi there, Mr Mountain,' Cheryl said. 'Do you think you could find somewhere for these? I'm even more loaded up than I was on the flight coming out.'

'I let her out alone just one morning in Paris and now I'm going to have to work right over the Labor Day weekend to pay for the damage. Not that I regret one red cent of it. Not one red cent – just the rest, that's all! Kidding, baby. May I introduce my brother- and sister-in-law, Mr and Mrs Bookman? This is Mr Mountain, Wes, took such good care of us on the flight out. Mr and Mrs Bookman have been on a honeymoon in Venice. Same time we were on our money-moon in Paris, isn't that right, Cheryl? Boy, is that one expensive city today!'

'Why not go the whole way?' Cheryl said. 'Why not show him your cheque stubs?'

'I'm not actually his brother, as a matter of fact,' Wes Bookman was saying. 'My wife is Mrs Shapira's sister, but Mr Shapira and I are not really related. We should have two in non-smoking and two in the smoking section.'

'Think he really wants the family tree?' Marsha said.

'How are we going to start out?' Cheryl said. 'The boys over there and the girls over here or what?'

'We can switch around, can't we?' Gabe said. 'It's an eleven-hour flight, minimum. We're bucking the Gulf Stream all the way, isn't that right, Mr Mountain? I just hope we get away on time. One thing I hate, it's sitting on the ground listening to people apologise.'

'Mr Mountain, do you have such a thing as a glass of water?'

'Didn't you take your drammy yet?' Cheryl said. 'I took mine at the hotel. You should take these things ahead of time.'

'I didn't take my second one and now I feel like maybe I'm going to need it.'

'Not too bumpy so far, Marsha.'

'Gabe, you leave Marsha alone. I have to endure your sarcasm; she doesn't. Soon as he gets near an airplane!'

'You two girls sit, nurse your hair-do's, relax; Wesley and I'll go smoke a cigar, what do you say?'

'Go and smoke your cigar. Put an airplane ticket in his hand and right away nobody can say anything without he starts being sarcastic. I hope you're not like that with Marsha, Wesley, when you've been married as long as Gabe and me.'

'Gabe and I,' Gabe said.

'You see what I mean? Now tell me I'm making it up. This is the last long trip I take with you, Gabriel Shapira, so help me.'

'Would you ladies care for something to drink before take-off?'

'No, thank you. I'll take my drammy and then I think I'll just – '

'You close your eyes, Marsha *mia*,' Wes said. 'It won't be long now.'

'Eleven hours,' Cheryl said. 'What's the movie? I bet we saw it already. *And* didn't like it.'

'I hope this was a good idea,' Gabe said, 'us all travelling home together. Cheryl gets like this before a flight. I thought travelling British might calm her down; those long 'a's are kinda relaxing. So Venice was O.K., right?'

'Venice was unbelievable,' Wes said.

'I can believe it,' Gabe said. 'We stayed one time on the Lido, which was nice, but kind of a drag when Cheryl wanted to go to the glass-works and stuff. Back and forth in the motor-boat all the time. Did you go to the glass-works? Fabulous. She didn't like it. Finally we moved to the Gritti, but the damage was done, you know what I'm trying to say?'

'We didn't leave the hotel too much,' Wes Bookman said. 'A little shopping, that was about it. We took in the square, nothing too demanding.'

'Got your exercise in the hotel, right?' Gabe said. 'I always knew that Roxana was a mistake. I knew it at the wedding. We gave you the vermeil forks, remember? Did you get those or did she?'

'I let her have all the domestic stuff. I didn't want to figure I was eating off a fork she'd used, even if it had been in the machine.'

'What kind of a name is Roxana, anyway, a Jewish girl from Sherman Oaks? I know exactly how you feel: take the forks and go. Shouldn't they be getting ready to close those doors pretty soon now?'

'Won't be long now, sir. Can I get you gentlemen something to drink?'

'I'll have a bloody Mary,' Gabe said, 'no ice. Same for Mr Bookman. It seems to be kind of full back there.'

'Full all the time now, sir, with the stand-by passengers.'

'Used to be you could stretch out, more space than in First Class. Now it's Disneyland back there, like one of the "E" rides, you know what I mean? Will you look at those two women, Wesley. I swear to God I don't know which of them is more beautiful. Ten years between 'em, who'd guess it with their clothes on? You shoulda seen Cheryl last night putting her hair-do to bed. She never moved all night. To look at her, neither did Marsha.'

'I like a woman keeps herself neat,' Wes said.

'One night you had to look but not touch, right? Well, one night won't hurt you. I'll bet she's something. I knew her when she was a little girl, but she still looked at you like she was making a promise you wouldn't be sorry if she kept. Am I right?'

'Marsha is a very warm girl,' Wes Bookman said.

'And a nice temperament. I'm not saying anything against Cheryl, because Cheryl and I've been married eight years and they've been eight good years, but Cheryl is someone gets very tense; she has a highly-strung nature, she can snap sometimes. Ping! I guess that's what I love about her: this element of danger. Of course she's a few years older than Marsha; Marsha could grow to be more that way herself. People do that, they get older.'

'Just look at them, aren't they something? Could be twins. I wouldn't be surprised they slept halfway to L.A. I hope they do. I want them fresh as paint at that airport, because we're going to have Max, we're going to have May and Bernard, we're going to have the whole *schmeer*. I could do without that, as a matter of fact, after eleven hours, but what can you do? Family! How's Leslie these days?'

'He's with his mother. I don't see him a lot. She's created a lot of hostility. He has kind of a weight problem, but he's O.K., he's fine.'

'Ladies and gentlemen – '

'It had to come, didn't it?' Gabe said. 'It just had to come.'

'Captain speaking. We have a small problem that's just come up. We're hoping it won't keep us long, maybe ten minutes, maybe a little longer, but of course we'll keep you informed. Meanwhile please relax, we're doing everything we can.'

'Sounds like two hours, minimum,' Gabe said. 'I know those ten minuteses.'

'Bloody Mary?'

'What's the story really, Mr Mountain, on this?'

'One of the baggage hoists is on the blink, sir, is all it is, I believe. We shouldn't be too long. Nuts?'

'Huh? Oh. Please. Always happens when I get here early. *Now* what the hell's going on?'

A young man in a polo-necked white sweater, knitted skull-cap and jeans was at the door of the plane which led on to the ramp. He was dark-complexioned and had curly black hair. He was insisting that he had to leave: he had forgotten something. The steward said that it would be very inconvenient if he disembarked now; the flight would have to be held up while they found his baggage. With the second hoist not functioning properly, that could mean a long delay. The young man said that he had just realised that he had left a vital book behind somewhere. He could not leave without it.

'How can a *book* be vital?' Gabe said.

The young man said that he was travelling only with a light bag (he held it up), so there was no need for any search. He just had to leave the plane, because this book was very important.

'He left his Koran in the hotel,' Gabe said. 'Can you believe this guy? I'll bet he's some kind of a P.L.O. fanatic just left his nerve in the toilet. Look at those eyes. A book already!'

'He wants to get off, let him get off,' Wes said. 'He has a right and furthermore who needs him? He wants to read, let him go to the library.'

'What is it, Gabriel? What's happening?'

'We're losing an Arab,' Gabe said. 'Don't worry about it, baby. Go on back to sleep.'

Unfortunately, the steward explained, even though the young man had no luggage in the hold, the fact that he had boarded the aircraft and then left it again meant that they would have to make a search of where he had been sitting and anywhere he might have gone in case he had planted something in the meanwhile. There would, the Captain regretfully confirmed, have to be a further delay while the security staff did their checks. He hoped that the passengers would bear with him.

'If I ever see that kid reading anywhere near Marina del Rey, I'll kill him,' Gabe said. 'That's the most inconsiderate thing I ever heard of.'

'All you had to do was offer to replace the book for him when we got to L.A.,' Cheryl said.

'Damn,' Gabe said. 'Why didn't I think of that?'

'I thought of it,' Cheryl said, 'and I've had two drammies.'

'The guy wanted off,' Gabe said. 'Why keep a gunman on the flight if he wants to get off? You want to spend the next week on the tarmac with Colonel Gadaffi? I don't. What's the story now, Mr Mountain?'

'They're just checking the toilets, sir, and we're hoping it won't be too long.'

'Because my wife is beginning – I can tell – she's beginning to get a little tense.'

'Would you like another cushion there, Mrs Shapira?'

'No, my hair... I'm just going to close my eyes. I have this tendency to migraine. I hope this doesn't precipitate something.'

'Did Cheryl ever figure it could be diet, her migraine problem? I know a corporate lawyer in Palm Springs, cured himself of terminal cancer with a diet exclusively of squash, Hank Dancy, do you know him?'

'Cheryl gets tension headaches. This has been going on for years. Ever since she had her nose taken care of on account of her sinuses. I don't think squash is going to help her any. Hank Dancy? I don't know any Hank Dancy. Hank Alpert.'

'Dancy. He advises some bright people. He advises Murphy, he advises Sheldon Franks. Hank Alpert is a shyster, someone was telling me. Do they really have to take the plane to pieces every time some crazy kid forgets his library book?

Hank Dancy's a *fancy* shyster, which is something else. I never heard of this on T.W.A.'

'The British are ultra-cautious,' Gabe said. 'I guess they're right. Better a few more minutes on the ground than a guest appearance as a hole in the ground in *Airport '80.*'

The Captain was speaking again. He sincerely hoped that they would be on their way within half an hour or forty minutes at the outside. 'I bet that means an hour,' Cheryl said. 'I bet that means an hour minimum. This plane is going to take off two hours late, if we're *lucky*. I knew we should have flown T.W.A. We should've flown T.W.A.'

'Relax,' Gabe said.

'You hear how he talks to me?'

'You want a magazine, Cheryl? You want *Cosmopolitan?* They have it.'

'You've been married eight years, he'll probably talk to you like that. Don't *ever* tell me to relax like that again.'

'Shall we try a little massage? Marsha, suppose you go sit with Wesley and I'll give Cheryl a little massage.'

'All you'll do is spoil my hair.'

'I won't even touch your hair. I'll stand behind your seat if you like. That way – '

'The back's too high. You've been smoking a cigar. You know what cigar smoke does to my sinuses.'

'I thought after that operation you weren't going to have any more sinuses.'

'Medically, you are so ignorant: I didn't have sinuses, I couldn't function oto-rhinally at all. Medically you're illiterate, Gabriel, you know that?'

'Maybe I should go get a book on the subject. Maybe that Arab could lend me one he isn't using.'

'I told you before about your sarcasm. As soon as I'm under stress, you can't resist it, can you?'

'All I wanted to do was give you maybe a little massage. How sarcastic is that?'

'I'm sorry, Gabriel, but I don't think I can stay on this airplane.'

'It won't be long now, madam.'

'I do not think I can stay on this airplane. I can't breathe.'

'Sure you can. Try some deepies. They look great in that pink angora.'

'You diminish me, Gabriel,' Cheryl said. 'Did I ever tell you that? You really and truly diminish me.'

'Cheryl, believe me, there's plenty left. I think you're the most beautiful woman for your age in the world. Now will you please relax, close your eyes and tell yourself – '

'Another couple of days in London would've done me a lot of good,' Cheryl said. 'Why did we have to fly home with Wesley and Marsha? They don't need us. Is there somebody you've fixed to see? I'll just bet there's somebody you've fixed to see. "For my age", what does that mean? Who is she, Gabriel?'

'She? She's a guy called Wallace Bergonzi, coming in from Albuquerque Friday. Coming in to see me about a property in Anaheim. They're just trying to take care of us, sweetheart, is all they're doing. She!'

'I feel terrible. I can't tell you how terrible I feel.'

'Cheryl feels terrible,' Marsha said.

'I know,' Wes Bookman said, 'I know. I think maybe you should go back and sit with her.'

'Gabriel can sit with her,' Marsha said. 'What's the matter? Don't you want me to sit with you?'

'I was thinking of Cheryl,' Wes said.

'Think of me,' Marsha said. 'I'm your wife, remember? As a matter of fact, I'm feeling a little jumpy myself. Those drammies, they settle you and they upset you all at the same time.'

'How about a little canapé?'

'I ate a canapé, I'd throw up.'

'It was squash, wasn't it, Hank Dancy took when the doctors had given him up?'

'Will you please not talk about food right now, Wesley?'

The Captain felt that he had to warn them, much as he regretted the situation, that there was going to be a further hopefully small delay because one of the warning lights was on the blink. They were sure that it was nothing, but they would have to get the engineers to run through the standard procedures.

'How long this time, for Christ's sake?'

'I don't suppose it'll be very long, sir. Would Madam like anything?'

'I'd like to get off this plane and on to T.W.A.,' Cheryl said, 'if you really want to know.'

'I'm afraid they've already taken off,' the steward said.

'That's exactly what I mean,' Cheryl said.

'Would you care for a magazine?'

'I already broached that,' Gabe said.

'As soon as there's any news, Madam, I'll come and let you know.'

'I doubt that'll be soon enough,' Marsha said, 'the way Cheryl looks.'

'Gabriel,' Cheryl said, 'I want you to be very understanding. I need all your understanding right now, because I have to get off this plane.'

'Cher, you heard what the guy said.'

'Which is precisely why I have to get off this plane, Gabriel. Now please don't treat me like a child – '

'You're behaving like a child.'

'I ask for your understanding and ... Did you hear yourself?'

'We've been sitting here for one hour and forty minutes, Cheryl, why crack now? We'll be away in a few minutes.'

'I don't get off this plane in about ninety seconds from now, I'm liable to pass clean out, Gabriel. Now please tell the steward to get that door open.'

'Cheryl's flipped,' Wes Bookman said. 'It was always coming. It's come.'

'We have to get her off the plane,' Marsha said. 'Believe me, I know that sister of mine. Better get the things together.'

'Come on, Marsha,' Wes said. 'Gabe can handle this, surely.'

'Are you serious?'

'We only agreed we'd fly home together at the last minute. We – '

'This is my sister you're talking about, Wesley.'

'Mr Mountain, I'm sorry, but my wife wants to leave the aircraft.'

'Mrs Shapira, is there anything I can do to reassure you? This is being done for your safety, believe me, and I'm sure it won't be long now.'

'I just want to get off this plane.'

'We're going to need our packages,' Marsha said.

'Come on, Cheryl, give it a few minutes, what do you say?'

'The Captain would like to have a word with you, Mrs Shapira, Mr Shapira, if you could just – '

'I'll bet we're all set,' Wes Bookman said. 'I'll bet we're on our way.'

'We were all set,' Marsha said, 'he'd have started his engines. Why do you always have to try and snow people?'

'I'm so sorry about this,' the Captain came through to say, 'but I do hope you understand. It's been a concatenation of trivialities today and I sincerely believe that there's light at the end of the tunnel. It shouldn't be long now.'

'I want to be in a tunnel, I'll take a train,' Cheryl said. 'Now will you please ask them to open that door? I have a right to leave this plane if I want to, and I want to. Now *please*.'

'May I just explain something? If you leave the aircraft now – which you have a perfect right to do, no one's disputing that – but if you leave the aircraft now, we shall have to get your luggage out of the hold, because if you leave the flight, we can't – according to international regulations – proceed with your bags on board. Given that we have this small problem with the luggage hoist, which I was prepared to leave as it is, since it won't affect us in the least operationally, your disembarking will mean a further delay of probably up to two hours for the rest of the passengers. So I wonder – with my most sincere apologies – whether you could see your way to resuming your seats to avoid that having to happen? In a few minutes, we could very well be on our way.'

'I wasn't trying to snow anybody, Marsha. See?'

'Will you please open that door, Captain, before I have an attack? Gabe – '

'She starts screaming, she won't stop. Believe me, I'm in a position to know. Mr Mountain, will you please open that door before I hold the airline personally liable?'

'It means unloading all the luggage, Cheryl,' Wesley Bookman said. 'We'll be a couple of hours – '

'Wesley, do you want me to pass out? Gabe can wait for the luggage.'

'Is that all our packages?' Marsha said. 'Do I have my *pâtisserie*?'

'I know!' Wesley Bookman said. 'How about if I stay on board with the luggage and see you all in L.A.? It'll save – '

'Wesley, do I hear you right? I can't believe my ears. We haven't been married a month yet, not one month have we been married yet! You stay with the luggage, my friend, and you stay with it for the rest of your *life*.'

'I'm trying to help, Marsha.'

'You stay on this plane and you never see me again as long as you live.'

'I'm thinking of Cheryl.'

'Well, think of *me*.'

'If you'd just leave Gabe to take care of her, there'd be no hassle.'

'She's my sister. You think I can do a thing like that? She's your sister-in-law.'

'She's a grown woman. She's been married three times. She's free, white and at least twenty-one...'

'I don't care how many times she's been married. When I've been married three times, I still hope she'll want to look after me. And what kind of a crack...?'

'Fine,' Wes Bookman said, 'fine. Lead the way. I'm sorry, folks. Y'all have a good flight now.'

'Traitor,' Marsha said. 'It's not our fault they let some P.L.O. freak on the plane in the first place. We were here before anybody. Everybody was like us, we'd be practically in L.A. already.'

'I'm very sorry about this, Mr and Mrs Shapira,' the steward said.

'The British just can't cut it any more, Mr Mountain, that's the truth of it. They just can't cut it any more.'

When the door was unsealed, the young man in the polo-necked sweater, the knitted skull-cap and the jeans was waiting outside. He was holding a large volume bound in red cloth boards. Close to, Gabe could see that he had a star of David on a gold chain around his throat.

'It was on the bus,' the young man said to the steward, 'wasn't that lucky?'

'Lucky!' Gabe said. '*Lucky?* You've wrecked our whole goddam trip. You've fouled up our whole European experience. You've probably destroyed these people's marriage and you talk about luck!'

'All I was trying to do,' Wes said, 'was make things easy.'

'Wesley, please, I just don't want to talk about it.'

By the time they reached the main building and looked back, the plane was already moving away from the stand. 'Holy Christ,' Gabe said, 'they're leaving with our bags. They're leaving with our bags.'

'Evidently we don't look like P.L.O.,' Wes Bookman said. 'The Captain decided to risk it. Well, thanks to us, the kid caught his plane. One man's sister-in-law is another man's *mazel.*'

'Terrorist,' Gabe yelled through the glass. 'Hijacker!'

Someone Else

Even at the university they had been marked for each other. (In the library, one could leave a slip in a book and be sure, in those days, that no one else would take or touch it.) At the white wedding, the families elected, in hired and hatted propriety, to regard them as innocents; their contemporaries conspired not to reveal what was common knowledge: that each had had a previous lover, though it had only been the other.

She did not take her first-class degree to market: she wanted children and a home. He went into industry and was industrious. He lacked her brains (said those who coveted her beauty), but he was vigorous and confident. Her friends announced that she was wasted on him, but she knew what she wanted, and needed. In perfect health, she married the right doctor.

That others thought them ill-assorted confirmed their complicity; their love was its own witness and they took private pride in it, as if in a separate creation. When Charles was born, he came as the customary cuckoo and displaced that earlier, honeymoon nestling, the talisman—aren't we lucky?—who had never woken them in the night (except to pleasure), as the newcomer did. She was not dismayed that the baby brought schism; she was well-read in the perils of the quotidian. When abstinence made him pettish, she was pleased to please him without tasting pleasure for herself. She drew the spurting sullenness out of him and smiled, with undisgusted lips, to see him better. He loved her for that soft succour, but its promptness was disturbing. How could she be at once so tender and so practical? It made her seem, for the first time, a stranger. He saw wit in her kindness and it made the first distance between them.

He was good at his job. Old Cantlie thought well of him and favoured his promotion. (They played golf together.) He handled people well and was soon showing the door, politely, to men who had shown him the ropes. His cheerful energy and undrawling accent belonged to no particular class: he could strip down a machine as well as he could ask Mrs Cantlie for a waltz at the annual shindig. ('I think they've done us rather well, don't you, this year?') His advancement seemed to incur no envy; it was only natural. He had his rivals (and liked them), but he had reason to believe that, among the raciest rats, he would win by more than a whisker. (Denton was the most capable of his age group, but one could not see him playing golf or chatting up important secretaries.) His popularity on the shop floor encouraged him to patronise the desiccated Denton (bright lace-up shoes, unfashionably tight tie); there was no spring in Vivian and the deciduous fair hair already promised a long and early autumn.

She went on seeing some of the brighter females she had known at university. Those who had disdained marriage rarely stayed unmarried, though their husbands—lecturers and publishers and poshish civil servants—seldom obliged them to live in a provincial town. Most of them continued to work, with fat absences for babies, after which they longed to get back to the office, frankly; breast-feeding, even in public places, seldom brought the promised thrill. Some of them sought to recruit her to their busy, full way of life. (Oh look, there was always proof-reading and indices to do for some academic!) She embraced the banality they guessed to be so suffocating. She had William and then Sarah. Others passed the age of thirty with sighs for lost opportunities and waistlines; she celebrated.

He thought that a junior directorship could not be far away.

Good old Cantlie contrived that he should have a car appropriate to the rank he could expect within the year. (This wretched
minor recession meant that a salary rise might have to wait.)
It was certainly no fault of his that the recession deepened.
He had helped to make the rather effective contingency plans
(he was number two on the subcommittee) without which
things might have been a lot worse.

When Cantlie was fired, at a week's notice, he had no
cause to feel menaced, though he was shaken. The firm had
been taken over by a larger, more liquid group quick to seize
its greedy chance. The old man's departure was as painful as
it was abrupt: the handshake was golden, but firmly final.
Cantlie's name vanished from office, car park and stationery.
One felt positively guilty, a couple of weeks later, at being
seen playing golf with the older chap on a Saturday. (Not that
those four-foot putts were easy at the best of times.)

The people who came down from London—and over from
Baltimore—reassured the work force that rationalisation
would not mean a reduced number of jobs. He was deputed
first to convince his union contacts that the new management
would keep its word, and then to supervise the reductions. He
was also asked, confidentially, which of the second-echelon
management he regarded as perishable: would he mark
them, for Harry Beach's eyes only, on a scale of, say, ten? He
contrived to upgrade—to a reprieving seven query plus—
several who had been proscribed by Denton, but he could not,
in the nature of the business, save them all. He was wounded
when a couple for whom he had actually fought rather hard
were easily overheard to call him 'that shit' at the gate one
night. He was hardened by their suspicions and frankly
rather wished now that he had gone over whole-heartedly to
the Harry Beaches and the Cyril Lacks. He proceeded to affect
towards them a bluff good fellowship he had earlier reckoned
either unnecessary or unworthy. He even clapped Denton on
the back as they went into a meeting and said, 'Well, Vivian,
m'boy?'

She listened to his stories, over larger whiskies, and winced at the stratagems of executive in-fighting. She had shared his scandalised amazement at the departure of old Cantlie (for whom she had recently cooked another of her bloody marvellous dinners), but she was less comfortable over the sudden zeal with which he elected to join the axemen, as he had earlier called them. She read his callousness as the symptom of a latent disease. Looking back, she saw its germs even in the intimate life she had, until now, considered so healthy. (His desire for her had been as regular as it had been passionate; now she saw in its clockwork heat a statistician's coldness.)

The situation in the executive building grew more anxious. Was there any end to the economies London (and Baltimore) had in mind? Every new concession proved only that not enough had yet been conceded. When several people were given notice whose jobs he had thought (and had said) were safe, he told Harry Beach that he had so much to do generally in the plant that he would be glad if he could resign from the steering committee. ('If it's more than you can handle, of course.') He came home that night thirsty with shame that he had tried so cravenly to ingratiate himself. After all, he knew more about the plant than anyone; even Denton had to admit that. His own position could scarcely be safer, could it? Imagine Denton trying to keep the brothers sweet!

She remained a patient audience, offering neither advice nor criticism. She applied her intelligence to remaining normal in abnormal times. However, she began again, in those chilling weeks, to do some serious reading. (The two boys were at school now and Sarah was no trouble.) When he came home one winter night, flushed with humiliation ('Nobody even *hinted* they weren't happy with me'), she put aside the journal she was flagging and went, almost with relief, to sympathise with what had surprised him but she had to pretend surprised her.

His collapse proved her strength; she could almost welcome it for the vitality it discovered in her. She was partner to his scorn, but not to his dejection; she bloomed. If she despised those whom he despised, the contempt was not new in her; she could simply express openly what she had always felt. No longer did she have to offer bright car-to-car waves to company wives or bend in Tesco's to admire dummy-mouthed kiddies; never again would she have to offer Sunday morning drinks to young execs who sat there and asked if there was anything they could do to help.

At first he was grateful for her resilience, but later it hinted at sarcasm in her that she took his wounds so bravely. The firm was not ungenerous in its severance payments (though he had to give back the car, of course) and they promised excellent references, but the employment market was not happy. There was a period of distant interviews, of stamped addressed envelopes (folded to fit in another of the same stock size) and of unreturned phone calls for which one waited all bloody day. Her resumed reading qualified her for part-time work in the field where she had gained her degree. He got to know his children. Her unexpected readiness to step into the breach made him feel that perhaps there had always been some weakness in his character about which she had kept a knowing silence. Her ability saved the day, but the nights lost their regular charm.

He was dashed, but not broken. He believed so strongly in his star that he insisted, even at its darkest eclipse, that the future was bright. (He was basically a lucky man who had had a bit of bad luck.) And after nearly three months of blue-suited anguish (always ready for interviews for jobs he did not really want), his old boss introduced him to some people who were hunting for his kind of head. They were manu-facturers of kitchen equipment and had a new infra-red operation, poised to break into Europe. It meant London and it also meant travelling. She would be all right, wouldn't she?

Of course, she welcomed London; it was convenient for what she was doing. The night before they left the cottage, when everything had been packed (the children were with the grandparents) and they were finishing drinks under the apple blossom whose fruit they would never eat, he wanted to tell her something. He turned his whisky in his fingers and thanked her for all she had done to see them through. She laughed and tried to cut him short. But they were leaving all this behind and he wanted to be shot of the whole business, to travel up to London clean.

There had been this girl. She was an ex-secretary. 'Do you have to tell me?' she said. 'Probably you guessed,' he said. 'Possibly,' she said, 'but I'd sooner not have the details.' 'There aren't any,' he said, 'I just want you to know that I love you. She didn't mean a thing.' 'Then why tell me?' she said. 'Because it didn't,' he said, 'and because it wasn't anything to do with you.' 'Ah!' she said. 'It was stupid and—I don't know—a bit sadistic, I suppose. I needed to hurt someone. Myself maybe. I love you—I need you—too much to hurt you, so—' 'Is it still going on?' she said. 'Going on? It never went on. It was this one time. I bumped into her in Oxford. Pure chance. She'd changed jobs. She didn't even know I'd been fired, it turned out. I thought she did. I wanted to—I don't know—prove myself, avenge myself. We walked into Lincoln and went into somebody's rooms. Mad! She used to work for Vivian Denton. Apparently he's a secret poof, did you know?' 'No,' she said. 'He is. Anyway, that was it. I wasn't actually sadistic with her, don't worry about that: I'm not Jack the Ripper or anything. I just needed it—it was the job, not you—and suddenly—there it was.' 'Why tell me about it?' 'I thought it might explain something—about how things have been between us. I know you've been worried.' 'And now I feel better, do I?' 'You've been so marvellous. I want to start again from now. Everything's going to be good from now on.' 'Good,' she said.

The new job went well. He was as able a salesman as he had been organiser. His side of the operation was divorced from manufacturing and he had a team of eight, all young and all eager to prove themselves to the parent company; there was none of the pettiness of Jack Horners who know themselves cornered and must fight each other for the plums. He did have to go abroad rather often, as he had feared, but he promised her that there would be no more Margarets. 'You don't have to promise,' she said. He suggested that they have another child (there was room in the new Putney house), but she was researching, for a rather impressive man, on the psychology of arson.

He told himself, and her, that his absences lent zest to their marriage, rather than interrupted it, didn't she agree? 'I think you're enjoying it more than you were until quite recently, aren't you, darling?' 'I think I am,' she said. 'Is there anything —you know—that's bothering you?' 'I don't think so, is there?' 'I'm very happy,' he said, 'don't get me wrong. Routine check! I just wondered if you were.' 'Very,' she said. 'Am I getting rather dull for you?' he said. 'Not in the least.' 'I realise this job —' 'What?' 'It's pretty mundane. Selling kitchens.' 'It's pretty mundane researching for Nikolai,' she said.

One day, at London airport, sitting in the crowded lounge listening to indistinct apologies for the delay, he met a man whom he had last seen at his wedding. (They had played college hockey together.) 'Hullo, *Gerry*, where are you off to?' 'I'm off to the bar, which is about as far as we're likely to get this morning by the look of the scoreboard. Strikes! Bloody stupid self-destructive nonsense! Care to join me?' They took limes and lagers to a newly swabbed table, brackish with wiped ash. 'Amazing bumping into you like this, after last week.' 'What happened last week?' 'Didn't she tell you?' 'Didn't who tell me?' 'I bumped into your wife in the White Tower.' 'My wife?' 'Assuming you're still married—she was having lunch at the White Tower.' 'I very much doubt it.' 'But I spoke to her. She was—oh Christ!' 'I think perhaps you've got the wrong wife.' 'Look, I'm terribly sorry.' 'Nothing to be sorry about,' he said. 'I don't keep tabs on where my wife has lunch. And memorable as you are, Gerry, it is conceivable that she met you without feeling obliged to pass on the happy news.' 'Look, I had absolutely no intention —' 'I don't know what you're talking about.' 'Oh well, fine in that case. Anyway, how's things?'

He told himself that he should have known. He aged walking to his delayed flight. The recent past, seen in sudden new light, was badged with luminous clues. He could not blame her. Had he perhaps even incited her to it by telling her about Margaret? She seemed to have taken it so well. Bed had never been better, but nor had it ever been quite so — what? — dispassionate. The blow raised no immediately remarkable bruise. He conducted his business in Munich with conspicuous good humour. The secretaries giggled at his German jokes and the wife of Fritzi Behr stood on one long leg, a deliberate hand on his forearm, while he repaired her heel. It was a salutary surprise to discover that he was more indifferent than he had thought. He found he could smile at her deceit and imagine a slow revenge. He was not vindictive in his fantasies, but there was always the chance that he would meet a fanciable woman. He had never regretted his marriage, but now he had the chance to repair the nagging paucity of his adolescent experience, didn't he? Yet he flinched from Inge Behr in the back of the taxi which — on her instructions? — had taken a long way round to the suburban house of the Herr Direktor. He returned home, after all, primed with a sort of vindictive fidelity.

Everything changed; nothing changed. What had been commonplace was suddenly trapped with duplicity. He did not challenge his wife, nor mention the meeting with Gerry (what the hell was his last name?). He made love to her no less urgently, but the gasp of her orgasm was an amusement to him and his own, later, was a smaller pleasure than the knowledge that she had been deceived. He schooled himself to be his old self and discovered in that detachment how death is the unsmiling tutor of life. He watched with killing admiration the care with which she prepared her excuses. How adroitly she almost made him responsible for her elongated absences! Unfortunately, she sighed, she would have to work a little later in the library, because he was going away the following week and she would be more tied to the house. The observation of her subtlety did not lead him to hate her. Sometimes, not least in bed, he felt so strongly that their love could be restored that cruel questions stirred in his mouth like nestlings. Only his exuberance was muted. He was more patient with the children. His long malice domesticated him.

One day he left his office before noon and went to the library where she worked. He waited in a telephone box until she came out for lunch and then followed her to a vegetarian restaurant, where salads and organic bread symbolised modern virtues: one could be slim and economical. He waited for her lover without any plan for violent confrontation. On the contrary: he quite treasured the prospect of seeing his wife a new woman, because of a new man. She glanced round and then she took a tray and helped herself to eggs and shredded celery and cabbage with sultanas. She looked at her watch and, after closing a torn shred of napkin in her paperback, began to eat. It was as if he had never seen her eating before (he hid, private detective, behind his *F.T.*); he relished her as entirely alien and he longed to approach her, the fool who cannot think of anything to say. He saw beside her the ghost of her admirer and yet there was no one there. He shared her fancied disappointment, quite upset with the man who had failed her. He kept his eye on the door, hoping for a flushed, overlarge person, ponderous with books and thrusting late taxi change into his pocket. She rose presently (no pudding) and went past him to the door. He thrust the *F.T.* pinkly into his mac pocket and strolled out after her. She walked springily along the pavement. The bunting of cheap clothing at high prices festooned the famous street; cheeky slogans and raunchy symbols were loud for attention. She was wearing low-heeled shoes and he fancied that she had a naturalness none of the other women, thrust up on wedgies and platformed boots, managed to attain. He followed her (she still tossed her hair as she began to cross the street at a zebra, shy thanks to the motorist who fanned her across) as far as the corner before the library where she was researching. He wondered if he could contrive to dodge round and get ahead of her, so that he might meet her by chance and be pleased. He was about to cross at right angles to her, so as to gain ground on the far side of the street, when she turned left and went down a side street. He frowned and, frowning, smiled, as if at a touching foible. He followed her again, at a slightly greater distance, and was barely in time to see the kiss before the pair of them disappeared into a doorway which, a moment later, he saw to be flagged with the names of tenants. Nikolai Pollak had the third floor. Staring at the names, he remembered Gerry's last name, Cartwright, and hated him.

He went home to one of her best dishes, the chicken with the cream and mushroom sauce. He ate with a good appetite and talked about his day, and hers. He had been promoted to the mini-board, responsible for the kitchen operation, and there was talk of a share option if the accountants could work something out. She listened to him with marvellous earnestness; he was more touched by the sincerity he knew to be false than he had ever been by her undivided devotion.

He came to be a connoisseur of her treacherous tact. She took such credible pains to deceive him painlessly that her cunning seemed positive evidence of love. His resentment was purged by a fatuous exhilaration. He had lost her, he feared, and yet here she was: why should she be so dedicated a caricature of fidelity unless, despite everything, she cared for him? Her deceit made her alive for him in every gesture she made. He was moved almost to tears by the sight of her (through the summer kitchen window) bending to put a dish away. Her shoes, worn by the weight of her heel but gilded with the remains of the maker's name where her instep arched over it, provoked in him a fetishistic throb. He began to tease her with treats, suggesting that they lunch for a change ('The White Tower? Why not?') or that they go down to

Glyndebourne (he favoured Mozartian opera, with its shameless swindles), and he tried to guess when her smile was secretly
dismayed by the ruin of her plans for Nikolai. She was rarely
irritated and never implausible. Somehow she crammed her
double life effortlessly into normal time. He never tasted her
lover on her body. She was as sweet as a girl. He could almost
persuade himself that Nikolai was not really her lover at all,
but then he remembered the kiss, and hated Gerry Cartwright
again.

He met an early girl-friend who had recently been divorced,
had re-married and was already thinking of leaving her
musician. Her availability struck him like a rank breeze. He
listened to her without enthusiasm and, when the chance
came, preferred to be faithful to his own delicious agony. He
made no arrangements to see Pamela again and ceased even
to chat up the girls at the office. When he went abroad, he
refused the standard round of night clubs and the promise of
a bit of spare. ('Everybody does it.' 'I don't.') It was obvious
that he was very happily married.

Patience became a way of life. Had there been a period,
soon after his confession about Margaret, when he had been
indifferent to his wife? (She had gone dull on him, fearing
herself dull.) His complaisance by no means entailed resignation. It was a phantom game with real prizes (never had their
sex life been so beautifully tortuous) and at times he could
believe that Nikolai was the dupe, not he. When it became
clear that she had not seen her lover for more than a week —
and then for a *fortnight* — he became so solicitous of his rival's
feelings that he deliberately stayed overnight in St-Étienne to
allow her some leeway. He found his life full at last. He had
feared himself shallow, but now there were currents plaited
into dark depths by the unstaunched confluence of love and
hate. He could never be sure which was guiding his sly
devotion. When he did something for her — the new kitchen —
what was the motive? He accepted her tiptoe kiss with
joyous suspicion. Nikolai was in the room for him as he

touched her breast and he had, in that common gesture, the greedy thrill of the adulterer. Without having another woman, he enjoyed another man's.

The weeks spread into months. He came to feign love so cleverly that he learned its language better than when it had been natural to him. He read books instead of magazines; he bought records. He became a different man. His counterfeit of love was so carefully nurtured that it began once more to take in him, like a graft, and in a stronger strain. In consequence, jealousy grew green again. He had schooled himself to control his dread when she announced — ah that delicious affectation of regret! — that she was going to have to go to some damned seminar ('Shall I come with you?' 'Oh darling, you'd hate it!'), but suddenly what had been endurable was fresh agony for him. He could not eat. He made no scenes and concealed, as best he could, the bite that tormented him.

One breakfast-time, she said, 'Are you lunching today?' 'I don't think so.' 'Then why don't we?' 'If you're not busy,' he said. 'When am I busy at lunch-time?' she said. He put down the *F.T.* and went to her. She was in her blue dressing gown, without make-up. He kissed her morning lips and the cuff of her ear. 'Where shall we go?' he said. 'The White Tower? Or Veggies?' 'You say,' she said.

He could hardly believe his luck when there she was. As she saw him come in, she raised one hand and tucked a shred of napkin into her paperback and put it on the pine banquette beside her. He kissed her unremarkably. 'I'm having an affair with my own wife,' he said. 'Can't you find anyone better?' she said. 'I don't think so,' he said. 'Perhaps you haven't tried,' she said. 'What do you think of the nut cutlet?' he said. 'Well,' she said, 'it's something you can get into your teeth, isn't it?' The blush told him that her remark was borrowed (foreign change in the lining of her mind). Had she dropped in front of him some deliberate clue, a handkerchief for Othello? Was there malice in it, or a gentle attempt to broach the unspeakable? He watched as she put slaw into her mouth. 'I love you,' he said. She finished her mouthful, eyes on his face, and wiped her West End lips before she spoke. 'Well, I love you,' she said. 'Do you?' She broke wholewheat bread and pressed the crumbs together. 'Something's worrying you. What?' 'Nothing is.' 'You're not eating.' 'Yes, I am, look.' 'Generally,' she said, 'so presumably something's worrying you. It's not the office, is it?' 'I worry the office,' he said. 'I promise you I'm fine. I'm nearly forty, you know. I don't want to put on lard.' 'There's nothing to worry about,' she said, 'I promise you.' 'Then I won't worry,' he said. 'Nothing,' she said, 'unless it's something you're keeping from me.' 'I don't keep anything from you,' he said, 'except my Swiss bank account.' 'Keep it,' she said, 'I'm not bothered about that.' 'I don't keep anything from you,' he said. 'We went through a bit of a time,' she said, 'didn't we?' 'Did we?' he said. 'It's over now,' she said. 'You've been so lovely these last — I don't know — months, I suppose, that I think I love you more than I ever did before.' 'Before what?' 'Before,' she said. 'Will you marry me?' he said. 'I can't,' she said, 'I'm married already.' 'Seriously. If we weren't married, would you?' She took the wadded napkin to treacherous eyes and nodded briskly, three times, and then turned and put her face against his chest and wetted his floral shirt, her favourite. He held her like a prize, while the rest of the room lost focus for a moment. 'I really am a lucky man,' he said, and blinked and looked to the door for a jealous face to spice his victory. 'I don't want anyone but you,' she said, 'not ever.' 'Good,' he said, deprived.

On the Black List

Matt Hyams drove into Torreroja on the afternoon of the summer *corrida*. Cars with red-lettered international plates were parked by the bull-ring. Donkeys and a couple of horses, with red-tasselled trappings and fat stirrups, were tethered under a spear-leaved eucalyptus tree. The bull-ring was the colour of old bread; the doorways and woodwork crusty with burnt sienna. Hyams had the window of the V.W. rolled down, his elbow jutting out, hand latched to the roof to make a breeze for his face. As he came by, the barn doors at the side of the ring were open and a furious-faced man was hurrying an old horse through them. It dragged a sidelong carcass. Hyams had a glimpse of crowded faces and caught the brassy vamping of the band. He had never heard of Torreroja, but it looked as good as any place else along the coast, so he pulled off the dusty *carretera* and nosed the bus against the wall of the new, starch-white church.

He climbed out and stretched. The V.W. bus was advertised for the whole family, but he seemed too big for it, even on his own. He had no family, not any more. He was over six feet three inches tall and he weighed two hundred and thirty some pounds. He was not fat; he was big. He wore size thirteen and a half boots (even when you were large, half a size made a difference) and he had on a blue Levi's shirt and off-white cotton trousers, baggy and creased from those six hours over the mountains. He squatted and braced his shoulders back: a one and a two and a three. He winced up at the sun and smiled, more grimace than greeting: he was working the stiffness out of his face. He had been wheeling into that sun ever since Granada.

He straightened up and ducked under the strung lights to go into the casino bar. The shutters were closed; two slow fans stirred the atmosphere like tepid soup. Heaped dishes of anchovies, olives and inky *calamare* stood on the long bar. A single customer, a scrawny man in a yellow linen suit, with a string tie, was prising open pistachios. Hyams put hairy hands on the flat of the bar and pushed himself up on to one of the stools. 'Beer,' he said.

'They call it *cerveza* around here,' the man said, though the bartender was already putting Hyams's glass on the bar. 'Did you hear the news? Hemingway is dead.'

' That's damned good,' Hyams said. 'Gimme another one of those, will you, please?'

'Near as dammit blew his head off with a 12-bore shot-gun. Did you know him?'

'No,' Hyams said.

'He came through here a couple of times. He loved to go to the bull-fights.'

'You don't say.'

'I'm Charles Larsen. They call me Chuck. Bull-fights give me a headache. On vacation?'

'Not exactly,' Hyams said. 'I'm a painter.'

'Oh one of those,' the man said. 'We have some painters in town already. Arnie Pallenberg? That's one of them. Wesley Van Groot? They come; they go. Me, I stay. I've been here five, going on six years. I was in Ibiza before that. Know Ibiza? It got to be so damned high, I figured it was time to move on. I'm on a U.S. government pension; ninety per cent disability. This is where the money goes furthest, so this is where I am. Were you in the service?'

'Yes, I was,' Hyams said.

'Ninety per cent disability,' Larsen said, 'and I never left U.S. soil. Climate suits me here; I've only got one lung. I got

T.B. in Fort Worth and they shipped me out – ninety per cent disability. I fought for a hundred, but they said, "Heck, you've still got one lung, haven't you?" I had to give 'em that. Thinking of staying a while?'

'I might.'

'Take a tip from an old hand: don't show your money around. They respect a man's not too liberal, if you understand me. You haven't told me your name.'

'Matt Hyams.'

'And I'm Charles Larsen. They call me Chuck.'

'You said,' Hyams said.

He was tired and one of these villages looked to be much like another. Why not stay here? Chuck Larsen introduced him to a Canadian called Spanier, who ran a fancy, foreigners' bar (the *Quijote*, of course) and a little real-estate agency on the side. Hyams was in luck: despite it being the month of July, there was a big old house available in the *José Antonio*. Folks had been coming, but they'd 'cancelled oot', the Canadian said. The house was in the middle of the village, so Spanier was sorry, it didn't have a view. 'I don't want a view,' Hyams said. 'I'm a painter.'

'He doesn't want a view,' Larsen said, 'he's a painter. I like that. I'll remember that. You hear Hemingway was dead, Spanier?'

'Blew his head off with a 12-bore shot-gun,' Spanier said.

'See what I mean?' Larsen said.

The house had double doors flush on to the dusty street, but there was a vine-shaded patio at the back. Inside, the big, cool rooms had checker-board floors and there was a long studio under the rafters, with whitewashed walls which would suit his work. He worked big. A woman from the village, Paquita Martin, went with the house; she would wash and cook and make his bed. He rented the place for two months, with an option to keep it on through the winter.

Chuck Larsen helped carry stuff into the house. 'I'm only

ten per cent,' he said, 'but here I am. Honest to God, I never saw canvases this big. You always paint pictures this big?'

'No,' Hyams said. 'Tell me, do you know this Paquita by any chance?'

'Paquitas are a dime a dozen in this town. But they're all the same,' Larsen said. 'They all tell you they've got four children and no money and they all rob you blind. She'll feed you well enough for four, and that's exactly how many she'll charge you for, as well. They all carry these canvas bags, you know, so you can never tell what they're bringing in or how much of it they're taking out again. My advice is, get her to do the accounts with you every week – and the first time around make like you aim to see every single used match-stick before you let her buy another box. I'm assuming this is your first visit *aquí en España*.'

'Not quite,' Hyams said.

'Torreroja, the red tower, that's what this village is called, you know. And red is right. See the church just now? Brand new, right? They burned the old one down. And the priest in it. Not that they talk about it. No, sir, they don't call this place red for nothing. Only village along the coast doesn't have a jetty. No jetty for the fishing boats. Know why? Because they're still being punished for that priest and that church. Franco won't give 'em a jetty, even if it is nearly twenty-five years since they barbecued that reverend. No jetty until they've paid good. He's got a memory and a half, that smart old bastard.'

'Thanks for your help,' Hyams said.

'*Tranquilidad* is what he believes in. You know what that is?'

'Sure do,' Hyams said. 'It's what I've come for.'

'No family?' Larsen said.

'No.'

'I have a son lives in Newark, New Jersey; engineer. My last birthday, he sent me two pair of socks. I'm fifty-one years old. They wanted fifty pesetas duty. Two pair of socks, fifty pesetas. Catch me! I wouldn't take 'em; I said they could send 'em back. Name's Howard. Mother chose it. Howard could have 'em back as far as I was concerned. I haven't seen him in ten years, he sends me two pairs of socks and they want fifty pesetas duty. Forget it, you know what I mean? Let 'em take you once and, brother, they'll come right back and try and take you again.'

'You've been a real help,' Hyams said.

'And don't be tempted to give her anything extra, Paquita. You heard what Spanier said: three hundred pesetas a month, tops. No extras. No matter how you watch her, she'll rob you anyway.'

Paquita was a widow, she said, and she had four children, all daughters. She was short and kind of plump, but she had the coal-black eyes and the red mouth and gleaming dark hair. She sang all the time she was in the house. Hyams began with very little Spanish apart from '*buenos días*' and '*por favor*', but he soon learned '*dinero*' (she asked for money with a little shrugging laugh) and '*corazón*', because it figured in all of Paquita's heart-felt songs.

He worked from nine till half-past two, when she would call out to him from the bottom of the stairs, '*Señorito, la comida.*' He would come down and learn the Spanish for a new dish: *boquerones* in crisp yellow batter, *paella* roofed with *pollo* and *gambas*. She grinned as he protested at the quantities she prepared. The *señorito* was a big man and he had to eat. '*Todo*,' she would say, and stood over him till he had eaten it all, or all he could eat. When he asked her to share a meal with him, she frowned and shook her head, the wrong suggestion. She stood in the doorway as he sat at the table in the patio, her hands on her hips, a tutelary frown on that humorous face. '*Todo*,' she repeated, when at last he pushed his plate away. 'Take it home with you, Paquita,' he told her, but she shook her head.

Her honesty touched him. He asked her to pose for him. She looked alarmed. She was no longer a young girl and she had nothing suitable to wear. 'Wear what you have on,' he said. 'I like you just as you are.'

'Oh *señorito*,' she said. 'Will it take long?'

He might have been the dentist. 'Not long,' he said, 'and don't worry: I'll pay you for the time.'

She came back the next day with a black lace mantilla and a big silver comb and a pair of red high-heeled shoes, which she had concealed in her black canvas bag. When the time came for the sitting, she piled the hair on top of her head, fastened it with the comb and draped the mantilla over the top. She sat in a cane chair and smiled. She did not have good teeth.

Hyams sketched her quickly in charcoal and then in oils. He had always had an extraordinary felicity. Envious fellow-students had said that he could get a stranger's likeness if he ran past his window. He could draw so easily that he had never been tempted to abstraction. His lack of modishness sentenced him to a provincial life, even before he was thrown out of his professorship. Nobody wanted figurative stuff in New York and unless you were wanted in New York, you weren't really wanted at all. He accepted that.

Hyams had enlisted in the Abraham Lincoln Brigade when he was seventeen years old. His father had been a Union organiser who was run down on a picket line by a bunch of strikebreakers in a big car no one ever got the number of. Matt spent three weeks in camp at Gerona and then they shipped him home again. After that, it was art school and then the Marines. He used to say he was the toughest marine in the Pacific; he mowed them down with his bare brush. He never even had to hold a gun.

When the Regents of the University where he was teaching discovered his unhidden past, he was dismissed despite having tenure and being a veteran. 'I'm afraid you're a veteran once too often, Mr Hyams,' the Dean said. He attempted to bring suit, but he lost. The Junior Senator from Wisconsin had them all on the run, judges included. Karen was great, even though she had the two children. She supported him in front of the Regents and she even went up to Washington and told someone that being an anti-Fascist didn't necessarily mean you were a Communist, because she was an anti-Fascist and she sure as hell wasn't a Communist. The man said he would do what he could, but what he did was nothing. Karen fought until there was no one left to fight, except for Matt. His cheerful virility, the unashamed bulk of him, became an affront to her. He refused to mourn: who was dead, after all? He was; they were. She could not forgive him for forgiving those bastards. He said he was a painter, not a teacher; maybe they had done him a good turn.

'I do nice work,' he said. 'I can always sell my stuff. What's to worry about?'

'Nice work,' she said, in the house where the telephone never rang any more, though they knew everyone in the street, 'nice work! They've killed you, you slob. You slab.'

'I never felt a thing,' he said.

'No,' she said, 'no. But I do. I feel it. You were a professor, I had a life. I had a community. I was alive. Now...'

'Maybe I'll never be de Kooning,' he said, 'but then he'll never be me. I can always sell my work is what I mean.'

'Oh in Peoria,' she said. 'In Miami maybe, to those drecky millionaires, but...what gallery's ever going to take your kind of stuff? It's dated, Matty, it's art teacher's stuff. I'm sorry, but you know that really, don't you? Don't grin at me like that. I'm tired of you grinning at me like that. You take it so lightly. Matt, please don't do that, you'll tear something. God dammit, Matt, I told you. Can't you understand? I'm through. I can't handle it any more. I'm sorry, but really, I'm through, I really am.'

He wanted to go to pieces. He tried drinking, but it upset his stomach. He threw up before he was anything like high.

He sat in the empty house and read newspapers. He told himself he would never paint again. He went to ball games and found he was sketching the players. He went back to work. His disgrace was not famous enough to hamper his sales. When he had a stack of pictures, he drove down to Miami and had a show. It was a sell-out. Karen's drecky millionaires commissioned portraits of their wives, their children, their lovely homes and even, once or twice, their lovely power boats. They were generous and hospitable and Matt was soon his old cheerful self. He even dated a couple of air hostesses and got spectacularly laid. He gave them charcoal sketches of themselves in the buff and they were so pleased they wanted to start again. Why not?

By the time the Junior Senator from Wisconsin had drunk himself to death, Hyams had got a bunch of money together and one of the millionaires wanted to help him buy a property. But the comfort he could now afford brought out the pain of no Karen and no kids. He saw the boys, of course, from time to time, but there was no going back. Karen had re-married. It was painful to be in the same country. He decided to go on his travels. He was not sure that he ought to go to Spain, because of Franco, but then he wanted to go just to spite the old so-and-so. He wanted to paint goats and olive trees and the faces he remembered, or thought he remembered, from those three weeks in Gerona, the faces of the defeated as they moved towards the border, the scandal of betrayal worked like ink into their skin.

He painted goats and olive trees and the face of Paquita Martin, whose husband had been killed on a merchant ship when their oldest daughter was five years old. Hyams painted Paquita's gappy smile and her hairy legs and her red shoes she could no longer wear in the village. He painted her when she posed and he painted her secretly from sketches he made when she wasn't looking, when she was scrubbing a floor or fanning the charcoal with that clapping, whickering noise the little basketwork fan made in her brisk hand. Paquita stood for all those women whose 'men had crossed the border beyond Gerona. Her husband had actually been hit on the head by a crane-arm, but there was no insurance and she was too poor and too ignorant to think of suing the ship-owners. Wasn't that Franco too? Matt Hyams liked Paquita's scowl, that covered her embarrassment whenever she sensed his eyes on her, like a sly caress, and looked round abruptly. He laughed once, when she caught him like that, and threw his arms around her. '*Señorito!*' she said.

'Damn right,' Matt Hyams said, and let her go.

The British and American expatriates of Torreroja did not greatly appeal to Hyams, though he accepted their society amiably enough, when he walked up to the casino bar after the light faded in the evening. He drank a glass of beer or sipped an *aguardiente*, stabbing at Ramon's anchovies with a toothpick, but he made no effort to belong to the groups that formed round Arnie and Gita Pallenberg or a seersuckered Californian called Fred Deedes, who had made a killing in Mutual Funds. He didn't even pick up a woman, though one day a dark-suited man in Malaga offered him a girl, very clean. He couldn't bring himself to go along.

He was surprised when Arnie Pallenberg stopped by the house. Pallenberg was on a Guggenheim and had a relationship with a gallery on Madison Avenue. He was short, bow-legged, balding and smoked cigars. He wore a Levi's suit and local boots, hand-made by a guy on the *carretera*. When he saw what kind of painting Matt Hyams did, he was fulsomely embarrassed. Trouble was, it wasn't the kind of work he really knew how to relate to any more.

'Don't worry about it,' Matt Hyams said.

'I guess I've moved on from naturalism.'

'Don't worry about it,' Matt Hyams said.

'I guess I'm too design-oriented at this point. I'd like for you to come round some time and see what I'm doing right now. It might give you some pointers. Gita pots, you know; she's very talented too: she makes beautiful things. Stop by whenever you want to.'

Matt Hyams did not stop by. He didn't want any pointers. He went on drawing goats and olive trees and the working figure of Paquita Martin. After a few weeks, his studio contained a number of studies of Paquita, the majority from his secret drawings. He turned them to the wall or draped them when she came up to sweep the floor. He was afraid that she would think he was taking advantage of her. Perhaps he was. She was a small, hidden passion with him, Paquita.

He never made any effort to check her housekeeping. He gave her so much every week and when she asked for a little more ('*Señorito*, the price of *boquerón*!') he never held his hand out for the change. He was working well, thanks to her, and he had never been a careful man. He left money around in the bedroom, partly because he never wanted weight in his pants when he was working, mostly to advertise to Paquita that he trusted her. He told her that she was always to tell him if she needed cash. He despised the conspiracy of foreigners who made it a point of honour to pay wages none of them would have dared to propose at home. At first, Paquita would not allow her daughters into the house; she would shoo them out and talk to them only in the street. But after a while they began to come inside. He'd hear the door bang. Then someone would bring a chicken or a bag of charcoal, her cousin Jaime or one of his friends.

At first Hyams did not consciously miss the missing pesetas. The small coins meant nothing to him; he never knew which was worth what, but it was the custom (Chuck advised him) to tip the postman when he brought a bunch of letters and Matt was surprised one day to find that all the change had gone from his dresser. Paquita was quick with a couple of pesetas for the old *cartero*, saying without a blush that it was the *señorito*'s money anyway. He grinned at her easy impudence, but she set her face against any acknowledgment that she had been caught out. He was not annoyed that the coins had been taken, but he was sorry that she could not make it the occasion for humorous intimacy between them.

While she sat for him, he tried to make her tell him the history of the village. She told him about the thieving gypsies and about the carriages of the *ricos* in the old days, but if he so much as hinted at the Civil War, let alone at so specific an event as the burning of the church, she stiffened and put away her formal smile. Once he sought to reassure her by alluding to his own abortive attempt to take up arms for the Republic. She was unable to understand a word of the Spanish on which, the day before, she had been congratulating him.

For a week or two, no further money disappeared. But the house was unusually silent. Paquita no longer sang. The lunches grew smaller. Hyams was more relieved than vexed. It did not occur to him to chide her for the modesty of portions which still gave him more than he could eat. Nor did it occur to him to ask for change from the weekly money. One had to allow, after all, for occasional extras, like soap and polish. He managed to improve her temper by paying her more than usual for her sittings. One afternoon he told her the story of Goya and the Duchess of Alba, how the great painter (of whom, she swore, she had not heard) had painted one respectable picture of his patron's wife and another of her '*desnuda*'. Paquita showed him the gaps in her teeth. The *señorito* would not want her to do anything shameful like that, would he? 'Not unless you want to, Paquita,' he said.

'A duchess did that?' she said.

'Oh, a duchess will do anything,' he said.

'Not here in Spain,' she said.

He did not tell her that experts considered that Goya had never actually had the duchess model naked for him. The form of the body suggested that he had imagined the nakedness beneath the pretty woman's clothes. When Paquita had gone, Hyams removed the black dress and the mantilla and the red shoes and painted the naked woman as if she were sitting before him.

Chuck Larsen came by the house. He was going to get married and he wanted Matt Hyams to come to the wedding.

'Who's the lucky girl?' Hyams said. 'Not Caroline Valenti?'

'A Spanish girl, from Malaga,' Chuck Larsen said. 'Her name is Fatima.'

'A Spanish girl! Wow. I take my *sombrero* off to you. Where are you marrying? In church?'

'It's the only place,' Larsen said.

'Then that's where you'd better do it. I'll see you right after the ceremony. I never go into churches.'

'I saw Paquita's children in the kitchen just now,' Larsen said. 'They're turning out to be the best dressed kids in town.'

'My best congratulations to your bride-to-be,' Hyams said, 'and I'll see you on Saturday. Where are you planning on going for the honeymoon?'

'We're staying right here in town,' Larsen said. 'I have my cheque due, first of the month.'

'Spanish girl eh?' Hyams said. 'They sure as hell better've left you with the right ten per cent is all I can say.'

Arnie Pallenberg told Hyams that Chuck's bride was a hooker from Malaga. She had two children, one very dark, to say the least, and no husband. She had a great chest on her and she was taking Chuck for every cent he had. She was nineteen years old. If Chuck tried to screw her, he'd probably have a heart attack and Fatima would have a United States pension for the rest of her long life.

Chuck seemed to have no idea that he had been suckered. He wore his linen suit and a big carnation in his buttonhole and he came out of the church with the girl on his arm as if he had just turned twenty-one. The foreigners threw rice and the Spaniards whispered and managed to keep a straight face and to giggle at the same time. They all went into the casino bar and drank enough quick drinks to excuse a lot of laughter and the usual ribaldry.

Arnie Pallenberg drank, but he did not join in the laughter.

'What's the matter?' Matt Hyams said to him. 'If Chuck wants to be happy, whose business is it?'

'You mean you seriously haven't heard?'

'Somebody died?'

'Damned right,' Pallenberg said.

'Matthew, really,' Gita Pallenberg said, 'you seriously haven't heard? Hard-edge is dead. It was in *Time* magazine.'

'Hard-edge is *dead*. How did it happen? Not with a shot-gun?'

'You think it's funny,' Arnie Pallenberg said, 'but I've been hard-edge for three years. I have upwards of a hundred hard-edge canvases all ready for my show when we get back to New York, and now it's dead and so are they.'

'No gallery is going to even *look* at hard-edge.'

'That *Time* magazine,' Hyams said, 'it sure can be a bitch sometimes.'

Hyams gave his small present to Chuck Larsen (a hand-made coffee set from Coín, with a brilliant vari-coloured glaze) and ambled back to his house. The Californian who had done well out of Mutual Funds had asked him to come to dinner in the new *finca* he had just built. He wanted Matt to paint his wife, or was it the girl he lived with. Matt had to buy gas before leaving town, so he went to get the five hundred pesetas he had left in the top drawer of the dresser in the bedroom. Only three hundred were still there. He might not have noticed, but the denomination of the notes was too high for the theft not to be obvious, even to him. He was not so much angry as hurt. He was humiliated by the blatancy of the thing. He was willing to be generous, but he would not be taken for a slob, or a slab. Monday, he would certainly say something.

Paquita listened darkly to his story of the missing cash. 'But who could have taken it, *señorito?*' she said, when he had finished.

The patronising endearment was too much for him. 'Who do you think took it?' he yelled at her. 'No one has a key except for me and you. I didn't take it. Now guess who took it. You got one guess, Paquita.'

She stood there for a few seconds. 'I'm going to my house,' she said.

'And I'm going to the police, god dammit,' he said. 'I'm going to the *Guardia Civil*, so help me.'

'I'm going to my house,' she said.

He grabbed her arm. He was strong and he held her. She endured his grip. 'You listen to me, you dumb broad,' Matt Hyams said. 'I told you: you need money, you tell me. You don't have to steal anything from me, not a *peseta*. O.K., you do it and I know you do, small amounts, fine, but this is too much, god dammit. If your family needs money, all you have to do is come and tell me. But this...Paquita, I – I *like* you, *comprende?* I don't want you to do this to me. I want us to be *friends. Amigos, comprende?*'

'I steal nothing,' she said. 'It was probably the gypsies.'

'You know better than that,' he said. 'If it wasn't you, who did you give the key to? Jaime? One of the girls? Come on, Paquita, I'm not just any one of those damned *extranjeros*, I'm an artist, I'm a man, I'm somebody who cares for you.'

'You don't go to church,' she said. 'You never go to church.'

'Holy Christ,' Matt Hyams said, 'the last time people were free to do what they wanted in this town, what did they do? They burned the goddam church down to the ground. They burned the *iglesia* down to the ground, right? Now don't tell me you're sorry. Don't tell me you blame them. Paquita, can't you try and understand? I'm on your side.'

'I steal nothing,' she said. 'I'm going to my house.'

'O.K.,' Matt Hyams said, 'Franco took the money. As a

contribution to the new jetty. Or maybe you think I took it.'

'You ask me to pose for you *desnuda*,' Paquita said. 'I'm going to my house.'

'Go,' Hyams said. 'You want to go, go. If you want everyone to know you're a thief, why should I try and stop you? Get the hell out of here as a matter of fact.'

She stood in the doorway with her black shopping bag and the shawl over her shoulders. 'Friends?' she said. '*Communist!*'

Sleeps Six

They always took a villa on the Mediterranean during the month of August. 'Mugs' month it may be,' Geoff said, 'but this mug can afford it. The kids're at home; Sherry and I keep it free and I can look forward to it all the year round.' Of course he did not lack sane advisers to tell him that he should invest in a decent little property. 'You could let it eleven months in the year, and the twelfth's on the firm.' Geoff preferred to hire his paradise than to be landed with it. Too many dream villas (look what happened to Jilly and Sambo) turned into nightmares from which their owners did not wake until local builders, and local vandals, had parted them from their last property dollar. 'I do not propose,' Geoff said, 'to become Madame la Marquise, and nor does Madame la Marquise!'

'Suit yourself, Geoffrey,' Philip Witham said, small feet, big desk.

'I do,' Geoff said, 'down to the ground.'

'Well, in your case it isn't far.'

'Christ, isn't it marvellous, honestly, Philip? How things've turned out? And a lot of it is thanks to you.'

'Skip the thanks, ten per cent'll be quite sufficient,' Philip Witham said.

'This year I'm bloody well standing you that holiday. This place we've taken sleeps six. The extra bedroom's off on its own, windows on the sea. I can show you the transparencies. They want a thousand quid deposit and they won't take it off just anybody. Six references! Stanley had it last year, he says it's a dream.'

95

'I'll take it,' Philip said. 'Only I'm never going to make it for more than ten days or so. I have got other clients, you know, even if I do keep them quiet.'

'We'll be there the whole month. It's yours when you want it,' Geoff said.

He and Sherry lived in a Georgian house in Chiswick ('I know,' Philip said, 'it originally belonged to a man called George,') with an alert staff from whose alertness, come August, they were not wholly sorry to escape. Big Annie was sent on a paid package with her mother ('Anything in the brochure short of the Seychelles, Annie dear') and Pontecorvo was free, in Geoff's words, to buzz back to Italy and flog all the petrol he had siphoned out of the Rolls during the year. Geoff drove the family down to the Riviera or the Costa Mucho. They stopped at all the places they had liked before they had money and liked even better now that they had.

Geoff had left school at fifteen to enter, as the year-books put it, 'the industry'. 'What did I do?' he would say to interviewing journalists who promised not to take much of his time, 'I made tea for the teaboy.' He had been industrious ever since. Before he was a producer, he was the best production manager in the business. Everything he had was paid for out of taxed income. If people thought it an immoral extravagance to live as he did, they were welcome to their opinions, but not to his drinks while they told him so. He had come from next door to nowhere (it was on the Central Line, if anyone was interested) and today he could pick up the phone and make a five million dollar deal before the pips had gone. He thought the tax structure in the U.K. 'frankly diabolical' (he was the director of a Second Division football club only three points south of the leaders and a mile east of where he grew up), but he liked it here. He accepted the bloody fool decisions of the majority until such time as he could get them changed. Sure, he worked for the Tory party ('Someone has to') and, yes, he did have an addict's taste for social occasions. He was at Ascot every year ('with a wife who can wear clothes like Sherry, wouldn't you be?') and they went to see Rodney at Eton on the Fourth, with a case of Mumm in the back of the Rolls and a quantity of Fortnum's canapés to attract the quality. Geoff was a generous host and an eager guest. He had had plenty of time in his boyhood to discover how the other half lived; he preferred the half to which he had now graduated. It amused him to have Philip Witham as his agent, but would he have stayed with his lordship if he had not been the best in London, as well as a peer of the realm?

Philip had been born into easy circumstances and made them difficult. He was sacked from his Public School for introducing a girl into the celebrations of the first eleven's victory over its traditional enemy (he scored the winning goal), despite his protest that they had been licensed to bring their own refreshments. He had subsequently been obliged to resign from the army after some trouble with, as he put it, 'the Jews'. He was a man of the eighteenth century born into one which, in the flat fifties at least, suited neither his morals nor his purse. After the army, he drifted around London and earned a fresh set of debts, which his father declined, this time, to settle. He turned for help to Gerry Pereira who happened to be in the process of setting up a talent agency.

'What's that, some kind of a knocking shop?'

'You have it precisely,' Gerry said, 'and you can play the piano in it, if you're good. It's about time you did something for your living apart from signing promises you can't keep.'

'I'll do more or less anything to get your Kosher cousins off my back, Lieutenant Pereira. Buy me a nice lunch and make me a proposition.'

'I'm not sure I wouldn't sooner watch you sweat, you fat *goyish* pig, but I'll take you to Wheeler's first. You've got just one asset, Philip, and that's your charm, what's left of it. It's something I might just be able to get to market for you before it goes off. I'll pay your debts, God help me, and then I'm going to ram your upturned nose against the grindstone until I see sparks. That's my proposition. Take it and you damned well won't leave it.'

'I hope they've got gulls' eggs,' Philip said.

They had been brother cadet officers at Mons when the foundation of the state of Israel was proclaimed. Some ass had made a jeering remark about its prospects. Pereira ordered a bottle of cheap champagne and, with proper and sudden ceremony, uncorked it in his unsubtle neighbour's eye. 'What I admired instantly,' Philip said, 'was your not giving the chap the ghost of a chance to defend himself.'

For all his profligate history, Philip had one undeclared vice: he was, in the right circumstances, extremely diligent. The scholarship he had devoted to racing form was now dedicated to the hurdles and handicaps of show biz. He became an assiduous and, when he had learned the silken ropes, a winning member of Mayfair Management. He was at once ornamental and effective. He did not give himself airs, but he dressed like the lord it flattered the clients not to call him. Americans were enchanted by his shameless vocabulary and his noble willingness to enunciate the unspeakable. (He told one producer that his client could not possibly come to Rome for the money suggested: 'I will not have him endanger his health by having to choose his women from the syphilitic side of the street.') He treated the business as a joke, which was why, being very business-like, he often had the last laugh.

Gerry Pereira introduced him to Geoff in the early days, when neither was anything much and Geoff was slightly less: he was coming up to thirty, married to Lesley-with-the-accent, and making a sorry living in television commercials. His unglamorous status did not prevent him from having half a dozen jejune projects: he had optioned a bad thriller and was waiting for a writer to do a worse script. He dealt from a deck of sweat-darkened visiting cards with 'producer' in dated italics after his name. He frequented pubs in Wardour Street and had coffee where others had lunch. He was trying all the old tricks, but he lacked the right rabbits and he had far too many hats. Philip found his naive ambition endearing; he found Philip an education.

One evening, after Philip had wangled an associate producership for him and they had been out for a claret lesson to celebrate, they were walking through Shepherd Market when a particularly dishy tart got out of a taxi just ahead of them. Philip conducted the negotiations. She led them—cantilevered tits, tightly waisted light blue skirt, flared over naked legs and high heels—up uncarpeted stairs to a well-lit room with a small electric fire. 'How do we go about it?' Geoff said.

'We toss for ends,' Philip said, 'don't we?'

Afterwards, they walked to where Geoff had left the Rapier. They made no spoken allusion to Polly either then or later, but if Geoff threatened to become pompous (success would put a bust of Napoleon on his trophy shelf), a reminding humour would flash in Philip's eyes. And if his lordship was too lordly (the new offices had a waiting room where some clients waited), Geoff's look could recall to him that night when Philip, finished, sat on the floor looking at Polly's printed recipes for resurrection while he himself went on to the final. ('*Well*, dear,' the girl said.)

In the street, as Geoff was unlocking the Sunbeam, Philip said: 'You really want to get rid of that wife of yours, don't you?'

'You haven't even met her,' Geoff said.

'That's what I mean,' Philip said.

He had nothing against Lesley-with-the-accent, but it needed no Pythian powers to divine that sentimental lust had propelled Geoff into an adolescent marriage he was now too squeamish to quit. Philip introduced him to Sherry Holland.

Sherry had been working in Mayfair Management, but she wanted a more responsible job. Geoff needed a girl Friday, didn't he? ('I need her Thursday,' he said.) She was tall and slim and had just come back from a year in the States (a cousin was a travel agent in St Louis). She was wearing a narrow black skirt and a white blouse, one button undone at the throat (coral pendant), when Geoff first saw her. There was a sort of intense modesty about her. She was very pretty but she was without vanity. 'She's actually much too good for you,' Philip said, 'but then so are most of the things you're likely to need.' In fact, not only did Geoff fall in love with Sherry Holland but — the long joy of his life — she also fell in love with him. 'I greatly distrust happy endings,' Philip said, when Geoff asked that he 'stand beside him' at the wedding, 'but what can a poor pander do? All I ask is that you allow me to choose your tailor before the ceremony.' (Lesley-with-the-accent had been primed to be properly indignant and sued for a prompt divorce.)

Geoff wondered, nudged by that realism which neither vanity nor sentiment could banish, what made Sherry prefer him to Philip. Why had she turned her back on a title and money in order to take up with a not yet established producer with a charmless background? 'I love you,' she said.

'I love *you*,' he said, as if there was a contradiction somewhere, 'I love you so much I can only say that I can promise you one thing—'

'Only one? Perhaps I'd better be going!'

'There'll never be anyone else. Not for a night. Not for ten minutes. Never. No matter where I go and you don't. No one.'

Philip was best man; the reception was at the Festival Hall (smart, but not pretentious) and they went on their honeymoon in the new Jag: 'touring', as the social columns used to say when Geoff read them in the Public Library out where Lesley-with-the-accent was holding the baby. They made their first contact with the Med during that trip; they had been going ever since. Their Augusts were celebrations of a marriage which showed not a scratch after nearly twenty years. Sherry was the foundation of Geoff's private happiness and his public reputation. 'If it weren't for her, I might well be the biggest shit unhung. But I can't swindle people during the day and go to bed with that lady at night. She'd know. I don't make dirty movies and I don't make violent movies; I'm a family man and incidentally it's the best investment I ever made.' He drove a Rolls and a hard bargain, but though he would always give you a lift in the one and keep his word in the other, he was perhaps too much the victim of envy (mother of I-must-be-honest criticism) to be entirely popular. People sneered at his social climbing and at the commercialism of his taste. When he put a Henry Moore in the garden, people said it was because he wanted to watch it grow.

Philip was as successful, financially, as his clients. He bought out Gerry Pereira in the mid-sixties (Gerry went to California to make custom-built cars) and under his firmly lackadaisical control Mayfair Management looked after the best stable of writers, directors and producers in the business. 'I'm not exclusive,' he said, 'merely greedy. I won't play nanny to clients still in their prams.' He seemed always to have time for those he did have: each had the impression that he was the favourite. When Geoff went to South Street, the telephone never rang in Philip's office; not a single file or letter suggested that he had any other clients at all. He was never in a hurry and he was always there before you were. What kept him so nimble? 'There's no exercise like a four-figure phone bill, it keeps you right on your toes, and other people's.'

His pleasures were as costly as his business, and less fortunate. He pursued his ladies with flowers, hire cars (he had never learned to drive, 'except a tank, briefly') and tickets to theatres and winter sunshine. He chose frequently and he chose badly. 'I have,' he said, 'a propensity for beauty at any price, and you know what the price usually is.' He craved fidelity from the faithless, steadiness from the flighty. He was on top of the world one week and ready to jump off it the next. The spare room (later suite) at Chiswick saw a succession of 'fiancées' whom Geoff and Sherry would cherish with optimistic attention. At first they regarded Lady Jane as no more likely to endure than Davina or Stephanie, though they were pleased that she appeared to have some genuine affection for Philip and she did actually volunteer to take something out to the kitchen, to which neither Vanessa nor Wendy, Nuala nor Miranda ever found the way. (Big Annie had Sundays.) Lady Jane was not the most beautiful of Philip's ladies, but she had a slow and humorous drawl and her blue eyes seemed to see something in dear old P.W. apart from the main chance. She was the daughter of an earl ('That's why I thought I'd bring her straight to you, squire,' Philip said) and she treated the expanding Philip with casual and correcting confidence. Her father had been in the cabinet, though not for very long, during the early sixties, and he was still counted in the Conservative party. Geoff was pleased when Philip asked him, over billiards in the refurbished garden room (the builders, like all builders, had almost finished), whether he was willing to be his best man if and when Lady Jane said yes.

She did so the night before they all had dinner at Cunningham's on the eve of Sherry and Geoff's departure for the continent. Geoff ordered a bottle of Dom Pérignon; Philip ordered more. When he rose to announce to the restaurant that he was the luckiest man in the world ('He can't be,' Geoff whispered to Sherry, 'because I am'), Lady Jane said, 'Philip, sit *down*, there's a good dog.'

Philip hung penitent paws in front of him and winked.

'You know,' Sherry said, 'it's going to be very difficult to know who to introduce my girl friends to, now Philip's going to be out of the running.'

'Introduce them to me,' Lady Jane said.

On the pavement, by the shining Rolls (Pontecorvo's parting gloss), they all looked forward to the tenth, when Philip and Jane were flying to Nice. Geoff kissed Lady Jane, Sherry kissed Philip and then his fiancée; Philip and Geoff shook hands, smiling. The entrance to Shepherd Market was just across the road. 'Many, many congratulations,' Geoff said, 'both of you.'

The first ten days of the holiday went so fast, Geoff said, that he thought there must be a hole in the month. The villa was merely sensational; it had its own pool ('Alison,' Sherry said, 'if you dive in much more often you'll wear a hole in it') and access, between exaggerated pink and purple bougain-villaea, to a tiny private beach, where they could laze and swim without any clothes on, impervious to binoculars. Geoff put the Ambre Solaire on a bundle of scripts ('essential in case the Chancellor shows up') and admired his wife's unfallen breasts. 'Nearly twenty years,' he said, 'and look at me: ready and willing.'

'Nearly twenty years,' she said, 'I suppose it's about time you were.'

'I'm looking forward to Philip and Jane, aren't you, darling?'

'Don't worry,' she said, 'it'll be fine.'

Alison and Rodney were playing tennis with some residents of Jersey they had met at a party on Bernie Pinto's yacht, so Sherry and Geoff drove into the airport alone. They had gin fizzes at the bar, while they waited for the flight and waved to a Peruvian princess they had met at Bernie and Bunty's. Sherry's eyes were shining, her shades on top of the springy hair, slim fingers enjoying the cool of the chilled glass. When the London flight was announced, Geoff said, 'Lots of time for one more. They're bound to be loaded with luggage they'll have to wait for. When a woman's going to take her clothes off on the beach, she generally brings plenty of them.'

Eventually they ambled towards the gate as passengers with hand luggage began to come through, going on tiptoe to look over and see if anyone had got the message to meet them. 'Christ,' Geoff said, 'here comes Phil.'

Philip was wearing a heavy blue pinstripe suit, a pink shirt and almost matching tie. He was unshaven and stumbled under the weight of a small attaché case. 'Oh God,' Sherry said.

'Fucking bitch,' Philip said.

'What the hell have you done now?' Sherry said.

'Not enough,' Philip said. 'Whatever it was, it evidently wasn't enough. Sherry, my darling, I want to sit down and cry and I want you to hold my hand. Where does one go?'

They had had Philip on bad days, and nights, but nothing compared to his present desolation. He smelt awful. He refused to be jollied or bullied from his slumped misery. He followed them about, in his pinstripe suit, sweaty and disconsolate. He almost telephoned his lady a dozen times and then flung the phone inaccurately into its cradle. They tried patience, they tried impatience. Nothing worked. Philip's capacity for self-mockery had been left in London. The children, who had always looked forward to seeing him, were prudently evasive. The weather turned grey. They had three days of lacrimose hell. Philip's socks became so smelly that he discarded them and wore his Jermyn Street shoes without any socks at all. Geoff finally had to order him to have a bath or leave the house. 'You're right,' he said, 'you're right, and don't think I'm going to forgive you for it. While we're at it, I may as well tell you something, I'm going to sell out. Mayfair Management, I'm selling out. They've been after me for it, they can have it. I'm sick to death of the bloody place. You've had fifteen years of my bloody life. I'm damned if you're getting any more. Nanny is hanging up her boots.'

'Oh for God's sake, Philip, pull yourself together. You're behaving like a silly old woman throwing crockery at the wall.'

'If I'm a silly old woman then I'm a silly old woman.'

'You're a silly old woman who's ruining my bloody holiday. I don't mind for myself, I mind for Sherry. I mind for the kids. Pull yourself together.'

'I've had my fill of that. I now propose to pull myself apart.'

'What the hell went wrong?'

'Did you ever tell the lovely Sherry about that night in Shepherd Market?'

'Suppose I call Jane and ask her to come on down here. Will you get a hold on yourself? You know she's fond of you – '

'Fond of,' Philip said. 'We're all fond of each other, aren't we? You're fond of me. What good does it do us? Did you? Tell her?'

'I really can't remember,' Geoff said, 'and I certainly don't want to talk about it now.'

'No, you certainly don't, do you? I should never have let you have her, you know that, don't you? Sherry. Shall I tell you why I did?'

'I think that would almost certainly be a mistake,' Geoff said. 'And probably a lie as well.'

'Shall I?'

'What happened, Philip old lad? Between you and Jane.'

'I let you have her because I thought you two suburbanites would set each other off to perfection.'

'Well, you were absolutely right, my son: we did, to perfection. Now, shall we have a drink?'

'Let's have a couple,' Philip said. 'And how did I know she was a suburbanite?'

'How did you know who was, Philip?' Sherry said, up from the beach.

'You know who, my pretty, you know very well. Because she was such a bloody prude, weren't you, in those days? Are you still?'

'I can't remember them,' Sherry said. 'But I expect you're right. You usually are. Do I get a drink? You sound terribly savage about it though, why is that?'

'Because I love you, of course,' Philip said. 'Oh don't look so bloody patient and amused, you bitch, will you?'

'I thought I was looking touched and sympathetic. You can see why I quit Drama School, can't you?'

'I remember looking at you at the Festival Hall at that ludicrous bloody wedding reception and thinking, Christ I've been a bloody fool. Why can't you have a row or something,

Geoffrey? Why can't you get kidnapped or something and I could comfort Sherry as she deserves? I am your oldest friend, aren't I?'

'You were. Philip's thinking of selling the agency,' Geoff said. 'So we don't really have to go on being nice to him if we don't want to. Shall we kick him out?'

'Kick me and I kick back, and probably bite and scratch as well. I had my colours for biting and scratching, in case you didn't know. Sherry, *are* you still a prude? You'd give me a kiss now if I asked you for one, wouldn't you?'

'Possibly,' Sherry said. 'If you went and had a shave and brushed your teeth.'

'Done,' Philip said, 'I'm prepared to close that deal right away. *Un seul baiser.* In my room in five — no, seven — minutes, all right?'

'It seems cheap at the price, don't you think so darling?'

'Doesn't concern me,' Geoff said. 'It's a matter between consenting adults.'

'I'll go and have a shave,' Philip said, 'and clean my teeth. And you'll be down, right?'

'Seven minutes,' Sherry said.

Geoff smiled at his wife, glanced at his watch and went into the villa. The children had decided to stay on the Pintos' yacht for a couple of nights. They were going down the coast to San Remo if the captain approved of the weather. Geoff took a script from the stack and sat in a loosely buttoned chair, Gucci feet on the matching beige stool, and took out his new glasses. Outside, cicadas were winding their watches for the night.

He turned a dozen pages and then put the black folder face down on his lap. Sherry came in through the now dark windows from the terrace. 'I hope you only gave him one,' he said. She bent down and kissed him on the mouth. Her lips were warm, her tongue promising between his teeth. 'And I sincerely trust it wasn't that one.'

Philip arrived, looking pink. He was shaved and he had

combed his hair. 'I've been an absolute cunt,' he said. 'I'm sorry.'

'Well!' Geoff said. 'Sleeping beauty! Cured by a single kiss!'

'*Un seul baiser*,' Philip said. 'You'd better go and change, my pretty.'

'Better call them first,' Sherry said.

'Call who? What's going on around here?' Geoff said.

'I've decided it's time to turn over a new leaf,' Philip said, 'and we're going to make it a gold one. We're calling the Oasis to see if a peer of the realm can persuade them to let us have a table for three. Never underestimate the importance of things people no longer consider important.'

It was difficult to get a table, but it was not, for his lordship, impossible. They drove into La Napoule, inspecting the unsteady parade of yachts tethered in the wobbly water. 'You know,' Geoff said, 'I'm not a carping man by nature, but it seems a bit weird old Bernie getting a life peerage when it's an open secret he's been avoiding tax on overseas earnings for the last God knows how many years. It's not illegal and I don't grudge it him, but it seems a funny carry on.'

'It's all a funny carry on, Geoffrey. Bernie's bilked the Chancellor with one hand and lashed out a hundred and fifty thou on his kiddies' ophthalmic unit with the other. Good luck to him. How else could he do it? And how do you think Jane's great-great-grandfather got to be an earl? Virtue? It was all on account of what happened when the Prince of Wales didn't have his armour on. You think there's justice? There's love and there's money and that's about it. In my case, the latter without the former, but what can one do? We're going to have a sumptuous evening and tomorrow I shall telephone London and get the invaluable Fiona to send me some clothes. She can put them on the next plane.'

'Tomorrow we'll go into Cannes and *buy* you some bloody clothes, you old Jew,' Geoff said.

'You ought to call Jane,' Sherry said, 'and tell her she's a

fool and she's to come down here at once. I'll bet you she's
only waiting for the chance.'

'Sherry my pretty, you may be right, but I'd sooner not
discuss it. Let her wait. We'll have a sumptuous evening and
we shall not look back for any reluctant Eurydice. Onward
and upward, my friends.'

Philip was as gracious as he had been surly. Yet Geoff's
gratitude was, for all the petalled excellence of the *mille-
feuilles de saumon*, more effortful than spontaneous. His
appetite was curdled: something in the script had disagreed
with him. Sherry smiled and laughed and leaned to touch his
hand as she proved to Philip how much she was enjoying
herself. Philip smoked a cigar and promised that he was
completely cured. 'Don't ever put your kisses on the National
Health, my darling. They're strictly London Clinic.'

They drove home in silence. Geoff thanked Philip for the
evening, with an effusiveness that proved how glad he was to
have something for which to thank him, and then went into the
big drawing room and resumed his script while Sherry got
ready for bed. She came in at last, in her nightie, and asked
whether he was coming or not. He looked at her through his
new glasses and said he would be there in a minute.

There was a note from Philip on the coffee grinder when
they went into the kitchen in the morning. He had woken
early and had decided to take the bicycle (there were a couple
in the garage) and ride into Cannes. 'We shall have the whole
morning to ourselves,' Sherry said.

'Yes,' Geoff said.

Philip telephoned at lunch time to say that he would not be
back till later, if that suited them. And later he telephoned to
say that, if they didn't mind, he might not return till after
dinner. Sherry came out and stood by the lounger where Geoff
was still working his way through the stack of scripts. 'We've
got the whole day to ourselves,' she said.

'What's left of it,' Geoff said. 'I wish he wouldn't bugger
about.'

'Well, if he's going to, surely it's better if he does it on his own. What do you want to do for supper?'

'I don't mind,' Geoff said. 'Do you want to go out?'

'Do you?'

'Last night was as much going out as I can take for a day or two, quite honestly. I wish we hadn't gone with him now. We could've gone on our own.'

'I'll make an omelette and we can finish the Brie.'

'I don't really want anything,' Geoff said.

Sherry said: 'Darling, what's the matter? Migraine?'

'All these bloody scripts,' he said, 'trying so hard to please. Shit with sugar, all of them.'

'Is it me kissing Philip? I wouldn't have done it if you'd said you didn't approve.'

'I didn't approve. I didn't disapprove. Christ, when you think of the business we're in, the way people behave. It's probably not that at all. It's probably the thought of Alison with the pimply Pinto boy. I don't know what it is.'

'Philip was being so bloody I thought it was cheap at the price,' she said. 'He said it'd cheer him up and, after all, at least it did.'

'At least or at most,' Geoff said. 'I expect you were absolutely right. Perhaps it'd cheer me up.'

'Come to bed then,' she said.

'We haven't eaten.'

'It might give you an appetite.'

'Sherry, there's no need to play Nurse Edith Cavell for my benefit.'

'Ah! Sorry.' The smile remained on her lips; the flesh stiffened around it. 'I'll leave you to your scripts.'

He read on for a while, lowering the script to his lap from time to time, but lacking the will to go in search of her. Silence filled the house like a Trappist's eloquence. After a while, he heard her come on to the terrace again. He put his espadrilles back on his feet and went outside. She returned his kiss but avoided his lips. 'Finished?'

'What did he mean about you being a prude?' he said.

'Oh! Beginning! I *see*. What did he mean when?'

'What did he want you to do?'

'What do people ever want young girls to do? Open wide, I presume.'

'Was there something specific?' he said. 'It sounded as if there was something specific.'

'Oh darling,' she said, 'please don't.'

'Why the hell did I have to ask him down here?' Geoff said. 'Everything was perfect till he arrived. He doesn't seem like the same person at all.'

'He is,' Sherry said.

They were in bed when the taxi drove up. Doors slammed and there must have been some mishap unloading the bicycle from the boot: they heard curses and a yelp and then giggles. 'He's got somebody with him,' Sherry said.

'He's got the driver,' Geoff said.

'Goodnight, Geoffrey,' Sherry said.

The girl was on the beach when they went down for an early swim, bright with determination to start the day afresh. She was wearing a pair of boxer shorts and plastic cups over her eyes. She was blonde and about twenty-three years old. 'Oh hullo,' she said, 'I hope you don't mind, only Phil's still snoring away and I thought I might as well. Chrissie Hollins. I hope it's O.K. if I'm here. You're Geoff and Sherry, aren't you? Phil told me all about you.'

'That was quick,' Geoff said.

'Sorry?'

'You're very welcome, Chrissie. Did you sleep all right?'

'I never have any trouble there,' she said. 'Lovely place. I hope you don't object to me not wearing me top, only I might turn a decent colour if I get some early sun.'

'Not at all. We rarely wear anything down here,' Geoff said.

'I've burnt the tops of my legs, that's why I put these on. My bum's bright red. If I showed it in the street, I'd stop the traffic. All I need now is to burn me boobs. I've never met a film producer before. I don't suppose you'd give me a part the way I look at the moment.'

'It would depend on the part,' Geoff said.

'Look, please don't mind me. If you want to go in swimming or anything. If I'm in the way, say.'

They swam out into the deep water where it was bruised purple by the reef that closed the bracket of the little bay. 'Nice figure,' Sherry said.

'And a nose you could open letters with,' Geoff said. 'What the hell does he think he's up to?'

When they went into the kitchen after their swim, Philip was grinding coffee. He had on a pair of pale blue shorts and a T-shirt MADE IN THE U.S.A. 'You've been shopping,' Geoff said.

'Did you see Chrissie? What do you think of her? Isn't she divine? She's the straightest thing I've ever met in my life. You're a silly bloody snob, Geoff, you know that, don't you? Lady Jane! This girl's the real thing. She makes me feel like a bloody schoolboy again. Three times in one night, no trouble! She's a fucking marvel, literally.' He put his arms round Sherry's neck and kissed her. 'His lordship's back in the race, my darling.'

Geoff said: 'What does she want for breakfast?'

'Same as she had for tea. These kids, Chrissie's generation, they're amazing. They've got a lesson for all of us. There's only one kind of sincerity that means a damn and that's the sincerity of the flesh. What do you want? What do I want? Simple as that.'

'That certainly sounds very simple,' Geoff said.

'Look, be honest, would you sooner I took her to a hotel? I'm perfectly willing. Only she was dying to meet you. Films, you know what they think of films, her generation. She's completely unspoilt. I'm going to change all that, of course, but for the moment, that's what she is. She does everything, Geoff, everything.'

'I'm very happy for you,' Geoff said.

'But naturally. Everything Polly did, in spades. For the sheer devil of it.'

'Who was Polly?' Sherry said.

'It none of it matters, old boy, that's what she's taught me. Liberation. It none of it matters. I'd better go and find her. She's very shy, you know, socially. She thinks you're bloody royalty. I'll go and give her a shout.'

'I wish to Christ,' Geoffrey said, 'that we could find a way of getting out of here for a few days.'

'Tell them to, if that's how you feel about it.'

'Be honest. How can we? We can't. Can he really not see what a grisly little tart she is?'

'Of course he can,' Sherry said. 'Why do you think he's so happy?'

The girl wore her boxer shorts and a pair of tennis shoes and nothing else, all day. She was, they had to admit, eager to please. She washed up, she brought them drinks and she certainly made conversation. If she was shy, she was not reticent. 'I hear you and Phil used to knock about together quite a bit,' she said to Geoff, while Sherry was doing something about lunch.

'Once upon a time,' he said.

'Your wife's lovely.'

'Thank you.'

'Considering her age. You must treat her right.'

'I try,' Geoff said.

'Do you mind if I take these trunk things off? Only I think I could afford a little sun again. I don't see much in my job.'

'By all means. What do you do, Chrissie?'

'I'm a telephonist, aren't I? Solicitor's office. You have to take what you can get. Phil says he's going to find me something better. I'd like to be a receptionist really.'

'Would you really?' Geoff said.

'I'm into pop a lot. He says he might be able to get me into something in music publishing. He says I've got the credentials.' She turned and grinned at him. 'You weren't always a stuffy bugger from what I hear.'

'Who's stuffy?' he said. 'And I'm certainly no bugger.'

'Give us a kiss, Geoffrey.'

'I don't seem to have one on me,' Geoff said.

'Trying to give them up?' she said. 'I was only being friendly. Is Sherry jealous?'

'No,' he said, 'I am.'

'I don't think I get,' she said. 'You've come a long way, haven't you, since you started?'

'Judging from the miles on the clock,' Geoff said. 'Not to mention the hours, and don't you!'

'She's beautiful, Sherry. Should I go and help her?'

'She said she was all right. Philip's with her.'

'He's been potty about her for years, only you're his friend, so he's not done nothing about it.'

'I don't think he'd necessarily have got all that far,' Geoff said.

'He told me about what she did the other night. I thought that was the nicest thing I ever heard, honestly. Oh look at that, my skirt's turning colour too! How about that? Me homespun! It's usually much darker.'

'I never heard it called that before,' Geoff said. 'That's nice! When do you have to be back at work?'

'I don't really,' she said, 'do I? Not now.'

'The great thing about her,' Philip said, when he and Geoff were watching the girls swim that afternoon, 'is that she's so independent. You might not believe it, but she's very competent. She was running her mother's shop when she was fourteen. Did the accounts, the whole thing. Her dad died when she was eleven. She's really had a rough time.'

'What kind of shop?' Geoff said.

'How should I know what kind of shop?'

There was a telephone call during the evening of Chrissie's second day. 'Alison,' Sherry said. 'The Pintos are taking the yacht to Corsica for a couple of days and they've got two spare berths. Do we want to come?'

'After protracted thought,' Geoff said, 'yes, please.'

They hoped that Chrissie and Philip wouldn't mind, but the children so wanted them to go on the trip and they saw so little of them these days. 'You and Chrissie're welcome to the place, obviously, and we'll see you when we get back.'

Bernie and Bunty were, of course, conspicuous with generosity. Bernie wore a cap with an anchor on it and was for ever going up to have a word with the skipper. He took the wheel when the automatic pilot had been set and he consulted the chart when the cliffs of Corsica were clearly in view. Bunty wore diamanté wedge heels and a trouser suit so badged with glitter that Sherry had to keep her shades on. They sat in chintz chairs on the scrubbed deck and were served with incessant meals. The Pinto children complained that there was something wrong with the cassette-T.V. 'The sweet smell of excess,' Geoff said, 'and I never needed it more.'

'You ought to get yourself one of these,' Bernie said.

'I lack your touch, Horatio,' Geoff said.

'From what I hear from Sidney, you've got the half-Nelson touch all right,' Bunty said.

'Sidney!' Geoff said. 'He should talk. And obviously does. I've got to go out to L.A. soon as I get back to London and all because of S.G.M. Bernie, tell me something about this Ophthalmic Unit of yours. I'm not in your league, obviously, but I do feel I ought to do something in the charity line. What do you think really deserves looking at?'

'Depends what you're after,' Bernie Pinto said. 'The big one, or just a knighthood.'

'I don't care about those things, for heaven's sake. What about Spastics?'

'More money than they know what to do with. I'll tell you what, if you're serious, Geoffrey, there's a man in London, ex-Colonel Coldstream Guards, you ought to go and see.'

'Lieutenant-Colonel,' Bunty said.

'He's got the whole thing at his fingertips. The Honourable Terence somebody. Lieutenant-Colonel. I've got his name downstairs. He's the fellow to get in touch with. Calls himself Colonel, doesn't he?'

They had quiet hopes, Geoff and Sherry, that when they returned to the villa three nights later, Philip and Chrissie might be gone. They were packed, but they had not left. Philip insisted on a last dinner in town. Alison and Rodney had been warned; they were tactful, but nothing could quite prepare them for Chrissie. When Norman and Dixie came by the table (Norman was scouting locations for a war picture from a command post in the *Hôtel du Cap*), Philip introduced her as 'my fiancée'. Chrissie's independence had apparently been overcome. 'And you know my best man, of course,' Philip said.

'How are you, Geoff?' Norman said. 'Congratulations.'

'What on?'

'Enjoy your dinner,' Norman said.

As they drove to the airport in the morning, Philip said: 'It's not going to be anything flashy. Just a few friends. You know how she hates ceremony. Only if you'd just do the routine honours, I'd be—you know—and so'd Chrissie, wouldn't you?' Philip turned and smiled at the girls in the back.

'Just tell me the time and place,' Geoff said.

'I love her, Geoffrey,' Philip said, head down. 'She's not Debrett, I know that. My mother'd have a fit. I don't give a bugger. She's what I want. She hasn't got a mean bone in her body. She's alive, Geoff, that's what it comes to. There's nothing you can't say to her. For once in my life, I'm not jealous even of you and Sherry. Don't think badly of me, will you?'

'Not unless you sell the agency,' Geoff said.

'Chrissie'd kill me. She's a businesswoman, Geoff. She's got a brain. She's clever. She was reading one of those scripts in bed the other night – during the intermission – and she made some very shrewd comments. Very shrewd indeed.'

'I'd like to hear them,' Geoff said.

'You and Sherry are my dearest friends. Always were. And now I have additional reason to be grateful. It's thanks to you I ran into Chrissie. If you hadn't asked me down here – made us feel welcome –'

'Oh shut up,' Geoff said.

'You can trust her, you know. She's open and honest, but she won't say anything she shouldn't. You don't have to worry. She may know, but she won't say.'

'Won't say what?' Geoff said.

'Those things just aren't important to her,' Philip said. 'If I tell her to keep her mouth shut, she won't dream of opening it.'

Chrissie kissed Geoff on the mouth when their flight was called. 'She probably didn't know you can kiss people anywhere else,' Geoff said, when they had finished waving.

'Bet she did,' Sherry said.

They had another nine days in the villa and they made the best of them, which meant that they were not quite as good as they had hoped. True, Alison and Rodney were with them again, content to return to the domestication which had earlier made them so restless. ('Nice to be back to Norman,' Rodney said.) Geoff and Sherry found themselves wondering, when they were alone (in bed or washing up), whether Philip had changed or whether he had always been like that. Geoff was uneasy at Sherry's indifference to Philip's fall from graciousness.

'I thought you liked him.'

'I do like him, but he's always been a shifty bugger, everyone knows that.'

'You're awfully nice to him, if that's what you think about him.'

'I like him. I said. But he's an opportunist.'

'In other words, you don't trust him.'

'I trust him to be an opportunist. Be your age, Geoffrey.'

'Not if I can help it,' Geoff said.

The telephone rang. It was (of course) Philip; there was good news, if you could call lots of money good news. Geoff had a pencil, put on the new glasses and jotted down some figures. 'I told them you might not be happy cross-lateralising it with the other picture,' Philip said, 'but otherwise it seems quite a decent arrangement.'

'It's very decent, Philip my dear, as well you know. Except that I'm never very keen on cross-lateral deals. They only come into operation when one of your horses takes a toss. Tell you what, tell them I'll agree if they'll raise our percentage by, say, five per cent, when both pictures are in profit. Try that one on them.'

'They won't agree.'

'In that case, fight to the death until you surrender. O.K.? How's Chrissie?'

'Something I wanted to ask you on that.'

'You already did, and I agreed. When's the ceremony?'

'Something else,' Philip said. 'Cross-lateral with that. She wants a job.'

'I thought she was going to work on you.'

'Do you think she could come and see you when you get back? She's no fool, you know, and she really took a liking to you. Father figure.'

'Thanks a lot, brother figure,' Geoff said. 'Well, of course, she can come and see me. What does she want to do?'

'Anything you want her to, roughly. How's the weather?'

'I think it'll last till the end of the week,' Geoff said, 'if we don't use it all at once. Anything else?'

'I think that's about it,' Philip said, 'unless you have.'

They drove home without haste, looking forward to Big Annie's welcome and the sight of Pontecorvo, mahogany with native sunshine, ready to resume custody of the Rolls ('Rather a nasty squeak in the cocktail cabinet door, Ponters'). They saw plenty of English cars but no English papers until they were back at the house. Sherry went straight for the gossip, Geoff for the Trades. Her news was hotter than his.

She brought him the *Mail*, folded back to display Philip in grey topper and all the trimmings. On his arm was Lady Jane. 'St Peter's Eaton Square,' Sherry said.

'I don't believe it,' Geoff said.

'Yes, you do,' Sherry said.

'He never said a word.'

'He may not have, but he's certainly signed on the bottom line.'

'He never said a bloody word. When did I speak to him? Wednesday. When he asked me to find Chrissie a job. He never said a bloody word. You know what it is, don't you? I'm not good enough for the bloody Earl of Stratford. I'll bet you anything you like that's what's behind it.'

'Not much of an arras,' Sherry said, 'if that's all there is behind it.'

'Who the hell do you think he got? As best man?'

'Gerry Pereira,' Sherry said, 'it says in the *Express*.'

'I wonder what the Earl thought of him.'

'I expect they enjoyed a joke together,' Sherry said.

'At my expense,' Geoff said. 'I'm not standing for it, you know. I shan't stay with him.'

'Oh darling, you know Philip—'

'I do now. I'm sorry, Sherry, but this is sheer malicious treachery, it really is. He could've told me. If he was in that much of a hurry, we could've flown home and sent Ponters out for the Roller.'

'He probably had to strike while the iron was tepid,' Sherry said.

'No, I'm sorry, it's a deliberate slap in the face. It's sheer bloody snobbery.'

'Oh darling,' Sherry said, 'you're much posher than Gerry Pereira.'

'I wasn't an officer,' Geoff said, 'and that sort of thing is more important to Philip bloody Witham than anything else, when it comes to it. And it's come to it. I shan't stay with him, I mean it.'

'I enjoyed our dawdle home, much better than going to some silly bloody wedding.'

'I enjoyed it too, but that's not the point.'

'It's my point.'

'What makes you so willing to forgive Philip suddenly?'

'He got lucky with Lady Jane and he thought he'd better tie the knot while he had his finger on it. I don't say he won't regret it, but you don't have to take it personally. He couldn't believe his luck; he grabbed it before it changed. I should call him up and give him a big kiss.'

'Like the one you gave him,' Geoff said.

'You wanted him to cheer up, didn't you?'

'It's a deliberate humiliation. God, when I think of that awful little tart and how nice we were to her! I spend God knows how many hours of my precious holiday pretending to be pleased that he's wished an illiterate little scrubber onto us, making her welcome, listening to her nonsense, commiserating with her red bum and finally agreeing to be best man at their wedding and then I come home and find that I've been — been —'

'Let off the hook,' Sherry said, 'just like Philip. If you're his friend you ought to be glad. You wouldn't want him married to her, would you?'

'And I've got to see her, I've got to give her a job. I'm fucked if I will.'

'Probably,' Sherry said.

'He knew then, when he asked me, he knew then it was all off. He's dead sly, you know, he really is. He takes a malicious pleasure in deceiving people.'

'Usually on your behalf,' Sherry said.

'He got you to do something, didn't he?'

'Who was Polly?' Sherry said.

'He even told you about that, did he?'

'He indicated.'

'They're shit, those people, aren't they, finally? The so-called aristocracy. Give me Bernie Pinto, frankly.'

'Birthday or Christmas?' Sherry said.

'He's a poisoner, Philip, and he always was. What did he get you to do?'

'You're a fool to go on about this, Geoff, you know.'

'If he fucked you, I'll kill him.'

'I lent him a hand,' Sherry said. 'Do you want a divorce?'

'Very modern of you,' Geoff said. '*Très* show biz.'

'I thought it was the least I could do.'

'I can think of less,' Geoff said.

'I didn't want the holiday buggered,' she said. 'Now do what you like about it.'

'That's what you wouldn't do for him twenty years ago, is it?'

'I suppose so,' she said, 'roughly. If I hadn't been so prim and proper, I suppose *I* might've been her ladyship. It's a thought, isn't it?'

'You still will be,' Geoff said, 'I promise you. You still will be. And we won't ask either of them to the party.'

'Just the Earl,' Sherry said.

You Don't Remember Me

'I know your face, of course,' Martin said. 'We weren't in Rep together, were we, by any chance? Worthing? Could it have been Worthing? I was there in '57.'

'No, I was never an actor, I'm afraid. Considerably less glamorous than that. It was the old Gloucester Club. We used to play sixpenny bridge together.'

'Good *heavens*, of course: the old Gloucester! Dear old Mrs Mac! Wait a minute, you're not Opie, are you?'

'Very close. Impressively close. I'm Opie's partner. Or I was. Opie's dead, you know. I'm Victor Milsom.'

'Victor Milsom, of course you are! *Dead?*'

'I'm afraid so. He died in Juan-les-Pins; well, in Cannes actually. We were playing in the Congress. Peritonitis.'

'What a dreadful thing! You played the Forcing Two, didn't you? With Ace Responses. Ruptured appendix presumably?'

'And Blackwood for kings. He thought it was food poisoning. We'd had some snails. We were lying second at the time. Do you still play at all? We get quite a decent game up at the golf club here, you know, especially at the week-end.'

'Golf! Now you're talking,' Martin said. 'I get a good bit of that in, when I can. Poor old Opie.'

'Ten years ago now. It's quite a decent little course; I play a fair amount myself, none too brilliantly, but...'

'It looks very pretty from the road,' Martin said. 'Is it very difficult to get in? Long waiting list?'

'I don't think a famous actor would have too much of a problem. Are you living around here now then, may I ask?'

121

'We've just acquired a place, as a matter of fact,' Martin said.

'Wait a minute,' Milsom said. 'You're not the Metcalfe who's bought Yardley Hall, by any chance, are you?'

'Guilty as charged,' Martin said.

'I was the estate agent,' Milsom said. 'We handled the place for Colonel Partington's widow.'

'Well, damn your eyes is all I can say! You kept very quiet about the dry rot in the tithe barn, didn't you?'

'*Caveat emptor*,' Victor Milsom said. 'Or hadn't you heard?'

'I have now,' Martin said, 'but it's a bit late in the day, isn't it? No, as a matter of fact we're over the moon with the place. I daresay we paid slightly over the odds, but today's extravagance is tomorrow's bargain, isn't it? And it had better be, hadn't it? We're thinking of doing up the barn and selling it separately. You could handle it for us, if you like.'

'Be a pleasure and a privilege. Are you planning to settle down in the country now then, after all your success?'

'*After*? Are you implying it's all over or something? Do you know something I don't?'

'Very little, I imagine. My wife watches you all the time, particularly that Film Quiz you do.'

'Meaning that she doesn't watch me when I'm Chief Inspector 'Arry 'Awkes?'

'You really should have been a policeman,' Milsom said, 'you're so quick at drawing the wrong conclusion.'

'Ah, a liberal! Do you live down this way yourself? Or . . . ?'

'Yes, it's just a modest little local business,' Victor Milsom said. 'I've been here for the best part of twenty-five years.'

'The best part of twenty-five years is nearly always the first five in my experience.'

'You've recently got married, haven't you?' Milsom said.

'We have regularised our union,' Martin said. 'The missus and I. Yes...'

'Sheila Armitage, isn't it?'

'Sheila Armitage it *was*; Sheila Metcalfe it is and evermore shall be. No, you're quite right. The last girl I saw you with wore granny glasses and home-made sandals and had one of the biggest shelves I'd ever seen. Out here, she was. What was her name? Mona?'

'Monica,' Milsom said.

'Yes, I wonder what happened to her.'

'I married her,' Milsom said.

'Did you really? I expect you were absolutely right. Well, look here, this is marvellous, bumping into you. We don't know a soul in the distict, we just saw the picture of Yardley Hall in the paper and down we came and... the rest you know. Really nice to see you again, Victor. What does one do about the golf? I mean, can I just turn up there and have a round? Are there any formalities?'

'It's open to the public during the week, on payment of the usual green fee – '

'Well, I daresay I could spring to that,' Martin said.

'But I'll have a word with the secretary, if you like. That is, if you're thinking of becoming a member. We can always do with a few famous faces – '

'I'll try and rally some of the clan then,' Martin said. 'No, seriously – '

'We have got a bit of a waiting list, but I am on the committee.'

'Are you indeed? Trust me to have friends in the right place! I'm not sure how often I shall be able to play, but obviously I'm most likely to be around at the week-end – we've got Sheila's old flat in town during the week – and it'd be rather a drag if one couldn't get a game on a Saturday or Sunday.'

'You can always play as my guest in the interim.'

'As soon as we're straight,' Martin said, 'you must come round and have a drink. The roses are still absolutely marvellous; especially those orange ones in the walled garden. Knock-out. And do give my regards to your wife. I'd've taken her off you, you know, in the old days, if I could, but you were obviously giving her the treatment she wanted. Poor old Opie, though, what a ghastly thing to have happen!'

'Yes, well, I must be on my way. Welcome to East Anglia!'

'Soon as we're straight,' Martin said, 'I'll give you a buzz.'

Sheila was arranging furniture with the two men who had brought the stuff down from London. She was wearing hand-painted sneakers and a pair of yellow dungarees, with her hair hidden under a green silk scarf. The men had the overweight agility common to their trade and their insolent patter was calculated to amuse but not annoy. There were tips to come. They greeted Martin with looks of flattering envy. Sheila had clearly been doing her sexy stuff.

Yardley Hall was a big, double-gabled yellow farm-house with Georgian windows and stone floors. It was too big for them really, but each had children from earlier disasters and they were not cottagey types. They could afford a certain grandeur, though they were determined not to be grand with it. The removal men treated them with an impressed familiarity to which, as actors, they were accustomed: everyone always felt that they knew them personally and fed them lines appropriate to the characters they commonly played on the box. (Sheila was always being addressed as 'dear Gwendolen', because of her Harrodsy part in 'Can I Call You Back?') The men quizzed them about the other people in their shows as they manoeuvred the baby grand into the long drawing-room: what about that jungle bunny Barry Coleman, Martin's Detective Sergeant in 'The Patch'? Was he really a Brummy or was that acting?

When the heavy stuff was all parked, Martin brought in beer and cheese and a jar of pickles, and they sat on the big hearth and had a picnic, quite as if the four of them were mates working for the absent owners. 'It's a bit of a giggle really, us buying this socking great place,' Sheila said.

'Nonsense,' Martin said. 'One should make a point of living in the style to which one is not accustomed. As a matter of fact, it's amazing how quickly you get accustomed to it.'

'Dead right, squire,' one of the men said. 'And good luck to you.'

'You see? I've come into my title already,' Martin said. The men accepted the spare bottles of beer and some of the five-pound notes Martin had been getting from the bank when he met Victor Milsom, and they all shook hands.

'Best of luck with it then, squire. See you on the telly, dear Gwendolen.'

Sheila waved them off down the drive and came back into the house, shaking her blonde hair free. 'Well, if it isn't the lady of the manor!' Martin said.

'And if it isn't, it soon will be,' she said.

He kissed those delicious lips. 'Welcome to East Anglia,' he said.

Monica was now a substantial matron, though she still wore sandals; she had had three children and the oldest was just twenty-one, studying engineering at Manchester, Ralph. She and Sheila spent the early evening going round the garden. Monica turned out to be an expert on pruning and layering and dividing. Sheila took large-lettered notes, with a big red and blue double-ended pencil. Victor and Martin practised chipping old golf balls up towards the gazebo at the bottom of the front lawn, under the monkey-puzzle tree. Sheila had cooked one of her *quiches* and they ate it with a bottle of Sancerre, followed by strawberries.

'We really should have asked you to supper first,' Monica said. 'I told Victor. This is all wrong really.'

'Not at all,' Martin said. 'We're the ones trying to clamber our way into local society and it's only right that we should make the first servile move.'

'Local society,' Monica said, 'I don't imagine you'll be wanting too much of that!'

'It's not as bad as all that, Monica,' Victor said. 'I'm secretary of the local Rotary, you know, and we've had some quite impressive speakers. I don't suppose – '

'*Victor*!' Monica said. 'He promised he wouldn't ask you till you came over to see us.'

'Oh don't worry,' Sheila said. 'Martin'll do anything for a round of applause.'

'Not to mention a round of drinks,' Martin said.

'You must get terribly bored with boring people asking you to do things,' Monica said. 'Or do you like being known as Chief Inspector?'

'Well, I was once dragged in to stop a race riot in Notting Hill by a black lady who absolutely insisted that I was the only policeman they trusted. I could've done without that, I must say.'

'And did it work?'

'It did actually. It wasn't really a riot, of course. Just a bunch of kids exchanging beer bottles at rather a rapid rate.'

'Chief Inspector 'Arry 'Awkes was hequal to the occasion, was he?'

'That particular one, yes. He was trembling in his oversize boots, but no one seemed to notice. They all came clamouring round for autographs.'

'I should think it'll lower the crime rate, just having you move into the district,' Victor said. 'Do you play bridge, Mrs Metcalfe?'

'Sheila,' Sheila said. 'No, I don't play anything, I'm afraid.'

'I'm going to teach her to play golf,' Martin said. 'It's good for the waist-line, darling.'

'If you did feel like coming along to Rotary one day, I know it'd be hugely appreciated,' Victor said. 'We meet at the

Dorothy in the High Street, not far from the bank. I'm afraid
we don't pay. It's just the honour and the lunch.'

'The honour's less likely to upset you,' Monica said.

When the Maxi had gone off down the drive, Sheila and
Martin took a walk around the dark garden. The tobacco
plants scented the quiet air. 'I rather like her,' Sheila said.

'Funny folk in the sticks! I'm not at all sure she always
knows what she's saying, you know.'

'And I'm quite sure she does. He's funny too. "Does it
offend you if I smoke my pipe?" People don't say those things
any more. And yet he's got quite a twinkle in his eye. You get
the feeling that they're going home to more than a cup of
cocoa, don't you?'

'God, isn't it super down here?' he said. 'I don't think we
should ever leave.'

'Why, are you planning to?' she said.

'Well, we'll wait until we've flogged the barn, shall we?'

'You go. I'm staying. It's such a relief, after London, living
among real people! What she doesn't know about gardens! I
can see myself being really happy, darling, you know that,
here? Truly.'

Victor rang and invited him to play golf the following week.
The course was much better than he had expected. It was not
up to Sunningdale or Royal Wimbledon, where the Green
Room Golfing Society played, but the turf was in good trim
and the lack of challenging contours was prettily offset by
narrow fairways and gouged bunkers. The little lake cost
Martin a ball at the fifth and challenged his spoon play at the
seventeenth, where Major Harper, the Secretary, clapped as
he holed his chip for a birdie after he had only just avoided
bombing the fishes for the second time. Playing level, he beat
Victor two and one but he suspected that the estate agent had
been discreetly hospitable. 'I really enjoyed that,' he said.

'Victor tells me that you're thinking of joining us,' Major
Harper said.

'If I can find anyone to put me up,' Martin said, 'I should like that very much.'

'You should introduce him to the Chief Constable,' the Major said. 'I'm sure he'd be happy to second you. After all, you're both in the same line of business, more or less, aren't you?'

They went into the club house and Martin played the sporting gentleman to the secretary's satisfaction over drinks at the bar. Molly, the barmaid, recognised him at once, though she refused to allow him to pay for the gin and ginger. 'Members only,' she said. 'Sorry, Chief Inspector, but you wouldn't want me to bend the rules, would you?'

'You keep your nose clean, lass,' he said.

Yardley Hall soon became the only place Sheila wanted to call home. Was this overalled gardening fanatic the same hard-drinking lady with the huge bill at Browns which had exasperated her ex-husband even more than her scarcely discreet affair with Martin? When the Chairman of the Parish Council came round to pay his first respects, she had him on his hands and knees in the greenhouse, trying to see what was wrong with the old hand pump in there. ('Nothing like well water, is there, councillor, for seedlings?') She was happy to reassure him that, of course, they could use the Hall grounds for the Fête next year as usual. The Rector came and congratulated her on her (actually Mrs Parker's) scones. ('What the *hell* did you talk about?' Martin said. 'Morals,' she said.)

Sheila even began to hope that dear Gwendolen might be killed off sometime during the next series, so that she could stay at the Hall right through the week. 'Christ, darling,' Martin said, 'you can't do that, we shall go bust.'

'You make plenty for two,' she said.

'I daresay,' he said, 'but I've got four, haven't I?' (Thelma and their son Christopher were living in Shepherd's Bush.)

'I can always grow things,' Sheila said. 'There's tons of money in asparagus, Mrs Parker was telling me.'

'There's a hell of a sight more in dear Gwendolen,' Martin said. 'You couldn't possibly do without London, you know you couldn't.'

'I know,' she said. 'I'll have it down for the week-end. While you're playing golf.'

He did the Rotary lunch (the second Wednesday of the month) and amused the guests with a few brass-type tacks from Chief Inspector 'Awkes, followed by some modest words from the actor who played him. Hawkes's fictional patch was an 'inner city'; his Detective Sergeant, 'Paddy' Laverne, was played by this black actor Barry Coleman, with whom Hawkes had a rather gritty relationship. 'How do you really get on with "Paddy"?' asked one of the Rotarians.

'We've both got a job to do,' Martin said, in 'Awky's gruff accent. 'We talk the same language on the job, we just don't 'appen to 'ave the same social life. Well, they're 'appier with their own, aren't they, if you're honest?'

'But how many people are?' said a voice from the back. 'Honest? What do you really think about the way they're taking over the big cities? Is the same thing going to happen out here, do you think?' Some heads turned, but most of the members recognised Bob Bailey and did not need to look.

'Oh come on, Alderman,' someone said. 'No politics!'

'It's a fair question to ask, I should have thought,' Bailey said. 'Unless you object to answering it.'

'If you do object,' Victor Milsom said, 'we shall quite understand.'

'No objection at all,' Martin said. 'If you want a straight answer, I should much prefer to be having lunch with Barry Coleman than with the gentleman who asked the question. In fact, I think I'll go and give him a ring as soon as I get out of here and see when he's free.'

Martin was sufficiently angry to be surprised when his answer was greeted with applause. Members were relieved to have a chance to rebuff Bob Bailey without actually having to say anything against him. When Victor proposed his vote of thanks to the speaker, he apologised to Martin for the 'embarrassment' he had been caused.

'I don't embarrass easy, lad,' Martin said.

'I hope that you'll bring Mr Coleman to have lunch with us one day,' Victor said, to some applause, 'because I know he'd be very welcome.'

'You didn't need to say that,' Martin said, as they took their cigars out into the early closed High Street, 'but I take my hat off to you for saying it.'

'I despise that man,' Victor said, as they watched the Alderman get into his Austin Princess. Bailey was a local builder; the red-brick shopping precinct opposite the Dorothy had been constructed by his firm. 'Unfortunately...'

'Don't take offence on my behalf, Victor,' Martin said. 'That sort of man's always going to be around, and he's always going to be in a minority, so let's not bother about him.'

'He's a very good actor, isn't he, Barry Coleman?' Victor said.

'He's a damned sight better golfer.'

'Really?'

'He nearly turned pro, but he decided to be an actor instead. Easier life. Well, it is for some.'

'I've had a word with the Chief Constable, by the way. He'd be happy to second your membership application.'

The Alderman's Princess was parked at the club when Martin next went to play. Bailey himself was perfectly civil (why should Martin have been offended?) and nodded across to the celebrity from the bridge table. Victor was puffing at his metal-stemmed pipe, frowning at the dummy like a man for ever condemned to make the best of a bad job. Martin shook his head when there was a call of 'table up' after Victor had surprisingly, and skilfully, landed his contract.

'I don't know what took you so long, Milsom,' Bailey said.

'I wanted to make it seem difficult, Alderman,' Victor said, digging for dottle.

Martin liked him.

When they started taping the new series of *The Patch*, he mentioned to Barry Coleman that he had joined a new club down where he was now living. 'Oh man,' Barry said, 'I know Yardley. Nice! I go past there on my way to Harwich. I've got this bird in Felixstowe I go to see. Very nice! I drive right past there.'

'Come down and play next week,' Martin said.

'Why should a player of my class waste his time playing with someone like you, bwana, that's what I want to know?'

'Get stuffed, Coleman. Do you really have to go to Felixstowe for it?'

'You're not looking for some sick leave, bwana, by any chance?'

Martin grinned and thumped Barry on the shoulder. 'What about Thursday?'

The afternoon was grey and it soon began to drizzle. Barry went round in sixty-nine, never straining, always giving the impression that he was merely practising, which he probably was. There were not many people in the club house when they came in, glistening with the well-being that comes of having done something conspicuously uncomfortable for no good reason. Major Harper was chatting with Molly as she lifted the grille in front of the bar. He shook hands with Barry, when Martin introduced him, and agreed to join them for a drink, now that Martin was qualified to pay!

'I really enjoyed that,' Barry said. 'Lovely little course.'

'Do you live near here?' the Major said.

'Not yet,' Barry said, 'but I'm thinking about it.'

'He's going to get the Alderman to build him a bungalow,' Martin said.

Martin took Barry back to Yardley Hall for supper. Sheila was wearing cherry velvet pants and a 'tarty top', black slippers. She had been bottling fruit all afternoon; Mrs Parker and she had sterilised fifty Kilner jars, and filled them. 'My God, Sheila,' Barry said, 'you'll be doing home hints before you're done.'

'Before I'm done?' Sheila said. 'It's too late for that, I'm afraid.'

'Barry's so impressed with the weather, he's going to buy a cottage in the village,' Martin said.

'Seriously, Barry?'

'We saw that old thatched place just across the aerodrome,' Martin said. 'They've been paying him in coloured beads till now but, with this new deal, he's got so much of the stuff, he doesn't know where to put it. Well, you must admit it'd be convenient, Coleman. You could give me a stroke a hole in the afternoon and still be in Felixstowe at night in time to stroke a hole or two there.'

'Cheeky bastard.'

Barry came back a week later and decided to buy 'Constable Cottage' (it was believed in the village that the painter, or at least his brother, had once stayed there). He met no obvious hostility; after all, he too was a celebrity. The excellence of his golf also earned him respect, though he was perhaps a little too good; such effortlessness smacked of contempt for those who could not so easily explode out of the steep bunkers and whose approach shots did not nibble the green and trickle to within a yard and a half of the pin. However, Martin was in little doubt that the club was proud to have the Chief Inspector as a member; why should it not be equally honoured to have his Detective Sergeant?

'You shouldn't force him on people,' Sheila said. 'It's not fair on them and it's not fair on him.'

'With a skin Barry's colour, nothing's going to be exactly fair, is it?'

'Don't you like it down here?' Sheila said.

'Sheila, for God's sake! What're you turning into? If

Victor's prepared to second him, I don't see what there is to worry about.'

Victor telephoned to say there was a minor procedural problem.

'Like they don't want a black member?' Martin said.

'No. But I'm sorry to say that there's an unwritten rule that no one can propose anybody until he himself has been a member for a full calendar year.'

'Unwritten, eh?' Martin said. 'Oh well, if that's the case – '

'I'll propose him myself,' Victor Milsom said. 'No problem.'

'Oh Victor, will you really? That's most awfully nice of you.'

'What are friends for?' Victor said.

Barry's name had to be posted on the bulletin board, next to those of other candidates, so that members might add their signatures, if they wished, to those of his proposer and seconder. Since most of the candidates were local men, with business or family connections, it was not necessarily an ominous sign that Barry failed to attract many other sponsors, though Victor's reputation was enough to secure a few. The main decision would be taken in committee. There the prospects were favourable. A plan was afoot to extend the club house and build an indoor swimming pool; to finance it, extra money was needed and there was general agreement that the entrance fee should be raised and the membership extended. The waiting list which Martin had been privileged to by-pass would be more or less abolished, though clearly not every hacker in the county could be admitted to the course. Such considerations hardly applied to a scratch player like Barry Coleman.

Martin was rehearsing a new episode of *The Patch* when Victor telephoned from Yardley. 'Bad news, I'm afraid, Martin.'

'Not Sheila?'

'No, no, no, but I'm sorry to say they've turned down Barry Coleman.'

'Oh for Christ's sake,' Martin said.

'They didn't stipulate on whose account,' Victor said, 'but I rather think it's Bob Bailey's. It seems that he's divvied up for the extension to the club house and he's put in a generously low tender for the swimming pool as well.'

'The dirty bastard,' Martin said.

'Yes, well, it went to a vote and... I couldn't take part myself, of course, since it was my candidate. It is a private club. The committee... I don't think there was anything personal in it – '

'No, well, that's not really all that encouraging, is it?'

'I'm not sure that I'm with you,' Victor Milsom said.

'If it wasn't personal, what was it? I could understand it if Barry had chewed holes in the greens or taken his shoes off and wiggled his toes in the bar, but as far as I could see, he behaved himself as if he were a white man, more or less, don't you agree?'

'It's all very unfortunate,' Victor Milsom said.

'I'm sorry?'

'There's a hell of a wind blowing up here,' Victor said. 'I said it was all very unfortunate.'

'Look, Victor, I have to go and arrest someone on the roof and it needs a bit of rehearsing. I'll buzz over and see you on Saturday morning, if I may, when I get down to Yardley again. Does Barry know?'

'I don't have his... I thought you'd probably...'

'Yes, I probably should. I'll see him tomorrow; he wasn't called today. Well, well... few are chosen, are they not?'

'I'm just as upset as you are,' Victor Milsom said.

'I'm not upset, Victor. A bunch of people like that, what the hell do they matter to me or anyone else? I shall have to resign, of course. I'm not going on playing there in circumstances like this.'

'Mr Metcalfe. They're ready for you, sir.'

'I'll see you at the week-end,' Martin said.

Barry laughed and laughed when Martin broke the news to him. 'Man, what does it *matter*? I don't have to look for places to play.'

'I know that, Coleface, but it's the kind of thing that makes me boil.'

'If I boiled at things like that, I'd have steam coming permanently out of my ears. Forget it.'

Martin drove down to Yardley on Friday night, very late; they had not finished in the studio until right on ten, and then there were drinks in the bar, the usual cocktail of euphoria and anti-climax. What was television? You did it and people recognised you in the street for as long as the series lasted and that was it. Yardley was a good hour and a half's drive, even if you played private eyes on the dual carriageway and let the Bristol have its big head. It was a sort of madness, rushing up and down like this, with the wind beating in at the windows to keep the alcohol from overworking. Was it really worth it?

Sheila, bless her heart, still had the light on in the bedroom window. She was reading a book on plant propagation which Monica Milsom had lent her. It was the perfect restorative: Sheila with her breasts above the turned down sheet and the technique of grafting open on her raised knees. The wind thumped and rattled the old house and Martin knew that third time he really had struck lucky. It was certainly worth it. Yardley Golf Club? Who needed it?

Victor Milsom was sitting over some papers in his little study, overlooking the willows. The Milsoms' house was an old mill; willows grew thickly along the stream. Men came and cut them to make cricket bats, when the wood was ready. Victor lit his pipe ('You don't mind if I smoke this, do you?') and looked at Martin with glinting eyes. 'I've considered the whole matter,' he said.

'In all its aspects?' Martin said.

'And I've come to the conclusion that you're absolutely right. We have no course but to resign.'

'Oh nonsense, Victor. Why should *you* resign? It's my business if *I* do; Barry's my chum and it's my fault that he's been humiliated like this. As a matter of fact, he thinks it's all a huge joke. He's not in the least bothered. Come on, man, you've been a member of the club for twenty years. You'll probably be Captain next year; I heard them talking about it in the bar.'

'It's a matter of principle,' Victor said. 'I was the proposer.'

'Only because I couldn't be.'

'That's scarcely the point. I was the proposer and my candidate has been black-balled.'

'From birth, old boy, from birth. It's not worth making a fuss about. This is your patch, Victor. You've made your life here.'

'It's a matter of honour.'

'Oh bullshit, man. It was only a bit of fun for me, proposing Barry.'

'Seconding him. I'm sorry, Martin, but my mind's made up.'

'If you're doing this for me, I warn you: I'm not the grateful type. Not only will you soil your own doorstep, giving me a bad conscience'll probably put an end to our friendship as well.'

'I've made my decision. What you feel about it honestly isn't relevant.'

'Think of Mona. *Monica*. She'll never forgive us. Besides, you know damned well you'd love to be Captain of that pissy little club.'

'That's no longer the point,' Victor said, tapping his pipe against the stone sill.

'Sleep on it,' Martin said. 'Don't do anything rash. And above all don't imagine that I shall think any the less of you. I probably won't give it another thought. I promise you Barry won't. Wait till the wind drops. No man can make a sane decision with this kind of stuff going on.'

As he drove off, he realised why Victor Milsom's eyes had glinted so strangely. He had been crying.

When Martin turned the corner into Hall Lane, he saw a dark cloud blowing over the hedge that guarded the house. He sneezed three times at the dust as he hooked the white gates back among the laurels. Just as he was getting back into the Bristol, he saw Sheila running towards him up the drive, legs splayed with the effort to speed along the gravel. She was crying and shouting, hysterical with the ghastly news he instantly guessed. 'The barn – ' she said. 'The barn...'

'I know,' he said. 'It's fallen down.'

'The whole thing,' she said, 'like a pack of cards. Martin, it's flat. It's completely flat.'

'*Caveat emptor*,' Martin said. 'Blast the man.'

'It just folded up and – there was nothing left of it. It happened right in front of my eyes.'

'Pompous little provincial poop. You know what Opie died of, don't you? Boredom.'

'Who was Opie?' Sheila said.

'Oh I forget now,' Martin said.

Private Views

Marsden sees her first in a Chelsea basement at a party given to celebrate the yellow-jacketed publication of Ferdy Plant's whodunnit. Its plot, according to a Sunday pseudonym, concerns a man whose wife is murdered, whereupon her secret life is disclosed. The husband who loved her comes to hate her with such intensity that he contrives, through patient ingenuity, to be found guilty of her murder. This post-meditated crime is declared 'unsubtly schematic' by the reviewer, who awards Ferdy only beta query plus, though deeming him 'newcomer of the week'.

The girl is with a married man who himself is later found murdered. His killers leave no clue and his wife remarries, happily. He is supposed to have been shot in error: two men of the same name live in his block, Harry Groves. As a result of the shooting, the other Groves's life is investigated and he is sent to prison for offences which might have remained undetected, had it not been for his namesake's misfortune.

When the girl goes over to join the uncritical circle round a stammering, eloquent critic, the married man drinks whisky, no water, side by side with the hired barman whom he knows from another time. The girl looks new – she can only be eighteen or nineteen – but there is something decided, and decisive, in her youthfulness. Though she is still at art school, there is no trace of paint on her fingers. Her beauty makes so little claim – since it assumes so much – that Charles Marsden need not hesitate to look at her. She is a goddess whose nakedness one will never surprise. She wears a long and susurrant dress of purplish, pleated wool, with a strict belt. As she listens to the wit, she holds a waisted *copita* of sherry, freckled with light like her own ferrous eyes. She never smiles.

Her unquestioning silence provokes clever answers; the critic fumbles for keys to unlock her humour. Her departure leaves him criticised. He has to pin the tail of his remarks on a donkey of a woman, who fails to get the point. The critic, whose name is Household, is one of those toadies so eager to please that he does not dare to say a good word about anybody.

'Well, who is she?' Marsden asks.

'Charlie, really, do you not know Katya Lowell?'

'I've been in Ireland, haven't I?'

He has recently come down from Oxford, with a mediocre degree. ('Frankly, I never expected to do quite that well,' he tells his mother.) He elected to read Mediaeval French only a month before his final examinations. Such flippancy suggests shallowness, but Marsden is more bored than foolish. His disdain for academic honours announces private means. He exemplifies that obsolete Oxford strain whose finest affectation is to delay allegiance until it can find a cause sufficiently lost to deserve support. Charlie sets his watch (an uncle's) with a relish for punctilious anachronism. Katya Lowell, first observed in a world of unfinished things (the pillared wallpaper is half posted in the flat), strikes him as uniquely complete, as if she had already come into her title. He watches her like a paraded *objet de vertu* as she goes over to the corner where her Harry Groves is agreeing with the barman. Unsmiling eyes make an appointment, for which they leave.

Marsden is not much up on women. He has enough friends – and friends of friends – for London to present no lonely problem. The party takes place in a spacious past when it is still possible to park in the West End. Marsden drives a Sunbeam Talbot, with a recognisable open roof. He has rooms in Vicarage Gate (Mrs Jump). There is no shortage of local company. Ferdy's brother, Theo, shares a flat with

Marcus Hicks just along the way. Jim Farber and Pip Lethbridge are up Campden Hill. Women do not come into their domestic lives, except to dust. If Marsden needs someone on his arm, he takes his sister, Camilla. As for bed, he prefers breakfast.

Marsden has not yet acquired his title or the Irish acres. He has some money from a bachelor uncle who spent most of his life, but not much else, in the East. He can afford to enjoy himself, and a happy few others. Marsden had difficulty only in filling his mornings, so he started to go to auctions. Marcus was working in Bond Street; they would meet for a fishy lunch. Marsden bought little and sold less. If the art market entertained him, he disdained to play it, except playfully. He specialised in English interiors and compiled a monograph which he refused to a publisher, though he did have it printed privately. He liked hidden things.

Theo Plant presages the end of a certain London period by electing to marry this Peruvian cellist of his. Marcus Hicks picks at early gulls' eggs one day before announcing that he is interested in a widow, a Countess as it happens. When Marsden congratulates him, Marcus scans his face for surlier reactions. ('Are you sure you're not upset?') Charlie replies that he is thinking of going to Tangier for a bit. A chum of his Singapore uncle has a house in the casbah; among the blues and whites and pinks there are windowless rooms, cushioned and carpeted, where one can arrange unknown visitors. Marcus Hicks is as sallow and narrow-faced as a knave in a black suit. He has long fingers, articulate bones in skinny gloves. The boss on his wrist is hairless as a button.

'Shall you mind her, do you think?'

'Theo's done it, after all, why should you be embargoed? She sounds to be quite a catch.'

'They are rather catching, you know, once you get used to them, the sex.'

'So I'm promised,' Charlie says.

'How's your father these days?'

'In health and in Ireland. Long may he remain in both.'

'Are you and Camilla coming to Potts at the week-end?'

'That was the plan,' Charlie says.

'Because you can meet her in that case. We're going down Friday.'

Potts is the small country house owned by Marcus's stepmother, near Leatherhead. Camilla and Charlie get lost as usual and have to put the pleated roof up over the Sunbeam; spring hail rattles like spilled pearls. Brother and sister are said to be alike. 'She has my nose,' Charlie once observed, 'but I'm lucky: I've got her eyes.' Rumours do circulate about them, but they alone know the secret: none of them is true. Their resemblance is so striking that even without scandal they have an intimate sense of each other. 'If we slept together, there'd be no call to wake up.'

The Countess is particularly taken by them, a dark-eyed woman, white skin, sharp nose. At dinner she wears a little black dress and a lot of diamonds and is garrulous with her hands. Her hair is new ginger and her mouth very red. 'Oh I am going to be such dear friends with both of you!' she exclaims. 'If Marcus – my very dear Marcus – allows it. Oh he likes you both so much, you know!'

'Oh, is she Polish possibly?' Camilla wonders, over the Sunday morning kedgeree.

'Oh I think she's probably rather attractive, don't you?' Charlie says.

'Oh I think she's probably *very* attractive.'

The Countess comes down late, washed face, blanched mouth, head in a bandanna. Marcus fusses around her and is short with everyone else. The couple leave for London before lunch, just as the weather is making the others look up: there seems to be a serious chance of croquet after all. The Countess is muted in her farewells. Her hands never say a word.

Charlie goes to Tangier for a week, ten days really. While

wandering for presents in the old town, he meets an Arab boy who has picturesque holes in his ragged clothes and a vocabulary of husky directness. They go to a café where men are smoking hashish. Charlie tries a pipe. He has his first sensation of being old as this old child watches him. Desire is done down by the solicitude he reads in the other's eyes. 'I'm tired of boys,' he says, tenderly. The boy offers to show him the brothels: he has only to say when. Charlie tips him well but neither touches him nor makes another rendezvous. He is late for dinner. The master of the house fears that he has had an accident.

Theo Plant has opened a restaurant, 'The Gunroom', where the best cutlery consists of swords and spurs. He features three or four entrées and crinkled salads, but the specialities are summer pudding and spring boys. On his return to England, Charlie buys some unusual sporting prints (in Essex, funny county) and delivers them to Theo at 'The Gunroom'. He finds Marcus Hicks dining with Camilla. The Pole has had a misfortune. She has used some suspect shampoo and her hair has fallen out. 'Not all of it, you understand, but most.'

'Poor thing,' Charlie said. 'Is she very low?'

'She is a trifle low,' Marcus said. Camilla looked particularly stricken, though her hair was very fine. 'She's turned rather reclusive.'

'I've told him it'll grow out,' Camilla said.

'Look here,' Marcus said, 'are you going to join us or what?'

'I'm dining unfortunately,' Charlie said.

'Will you be home later?'

'I do hope to be home later.'

Charlie is drinking tea with Mrs Jump at soon after midnight when the bell rings. It is Marcus, and Camilla. 'Not to put too fine a point on it, my dear Charlie, Camilla and I propose to get married. I hope you're not going to be upset.'

'Why,' Charlie says, 'have you got plans for me?'

'It's rather sudden, though it doesn't feel so.'

'What about the Countess?'

'There is certainly that,' Marcus says, 'which is partly why we've come round.'

'I'm to be uncle Charlie, am I?'

'She likes you awfully,' Marcus says, taking a sudden demotion to the fifth form. 'And I wondered...'

'You really want to marry him?' Charlie says.

'Well, he asked me, didn't he?' Camilla says. 'And I've always liked his hands.' Her eyes allude to that bare boss on Marcus's hairy wrist and Charlie observes a strange gleam above his sister's mouth, a glaze of desire like a ghostly moustache. Now that she is beyond him, he rather wishes they had done all the things rumour proposed.

He goes the next morning to see the Countess. He buys some magazines to cheer her up. In one of them he finds a picture of Katya Lowell, unsmilingly enjoying a joke. The critic is wincing behind her, in a velvet smoking jacket; smoke gets in his eyes. The Countess seems scarcely to remember Charlie. She still wears a bandanna tight around her head and her face is bland of make-up. At first she is disposed to believe that Charlie has engineered the engagement between his sister and Marcus. They sit in the room overlooking the park with as little to say to each other as common patients in a waiting-room. Charlie has his magazines in front of him. He is tactful to begin with and then, when the Countess's reproachful eyes sweep him for the eighth or ninth time, he loses patience. 'I didn't pull your bloody hair out, you know.'

'Oh he was so kind to me,' she says. 'That is how I knew.'

'Knew what?'

'That he was going to leave me.'

'You wouldn't have been happy,' Charlie says. 'You've had an escape really, you know. Marcus would have led you an awful dance.'

'Oh I know,' she says. 'Do you think I don't know? I know.'

'Rather what you wanted, I presume.'

'What do you know about it?' she says, but nicely.

'I'll bet you it doesn't matter a damn,' Charlie says, quickened.

'What is that?'

'Your hair. Show me.'

'I have none. *None.* I have none. Not a blade.'

'A blade! Show me. I'll bet you it doesn't detract in the least.'

She looks at him with widely awakened eyes and goes and locks the drawing-room door. She stands in front of him and unlatches the bandanna. Her head is small and white, like a peeled vegetable. The ears are delicious. Her eyes accuse Charlie, not of what has happened, but of what he wants. He kisses the chalky lips until they redden. 'I think we have a future,' he says. 'Why don't you dispense with the rest?'

Her breasts are blue cheese to Charlie's uninitiated eyes, but they ripen to loveliness when she discloses, abruptly, the hair she still possesses, in abundance. 'There,' she says. 'That is a woman. Now you know what a woman is.'

Marsden leaves her the magazines, except for the one with Katya Lowell in it. That he takes back to Mrs Jump's. All the Countess's hair has grown again by the time that Camilla and Marcus are married, but Charlie likes her to hide it, so she still binds it under a bandanna. His desire is aroused, when they are alone, by unwinding the turban and allowing her hair to fall over the white ears. Charlie resists the temptation to move in with her, though he visits her roughly every day.

Jim Farber has decided to open a small gallery. One of the first artists to whom he gives a show is Katya Lowell. Charlie has put a pound or two into the place and goes to the *vernissage.* She seems unchanged, though it is several years since Chelsea. (The married man is dead.) She is wearing a belted green dress, scooped out at the neck, but chaste with a drawstring. Her strapped feet are bare and brown in

Florentine sandals. She accepts congratulations with an unsmiling nod, as if she were acknowledging a joke she has heard before. Charlie does not speak to her and soon leaves to go and see Anya.

However, he returns the next day. Several of the pictures have been sold. Red stars confirm their desirability, as wedding rings can that of certain women. Her paintings are English interiors. Some bear the names of people: David, Iris, Wendy and Gavin, Miles, Harry. But there are no people in them. Another sequence is anonymous. The paintings are entitled merely 'His Place', 'The Flat', 'Punishment' and 'Scene of the Crime'. Charlie stands for some time in front of 'Punishment'. Jim Farber has been busy on the telephone, to Brussels, but comes, bearded, to stand beside him. 'I like her paint,' Charlie says at last. Jim Farber is slightly older than Charlie. They were at school together and Jim punished his junior two or three times.

The room was clean, the paint without impasto. A round, gate-legged table (one leaf autumnal) was laid for breakfast under a window looking deep into a garden pricked with daffodils. The garden was no larger than half a postcard; the daffodils, pin-high, were depicted in subtle counter-perspective. In the foreground was a Windsor chair, a dress laid across it. Charlie recognised the purplish wool, a date from an old diary. The belt was over the back. There was a red star in the corner of the canvas.

'I realise it's not normally done,' Charlie says, 'but could I possibly know who bought it?'

That evening he gave notice to Mrs Jump. He was awfully sorry but he had decided to find a place of his own. He rejected several flats which the agent, personally recommended by Theo, proposed to him. He had finally to take the young man to the Farber gallery, to show him exactly what he wanted. 'And I do mean exactly.'

'It's going to have to be rather large in that case, isn't it, sir?'

'Oh yes, it is.'

'Are you getting married, sir, may I ask?'

'Of course,' Charlie said.

It was his culminating act of dandyism, the flat. He told himself, and no one else, that his decision to decorate it according to the prescriptions posted in the Farber Gallery was a capping caprice. After this, he would lead a normal life. He even proposed to take a job. Most of his friends now worked; there was practically no one to see in the mornings, if one was not to go on going to Bond Street. Pip Lethbridge (who had met a ballerina, just as she was hanging up her shoes) introduced him to these people in the City. The prospect of being employed by Norwegians amused him rather, so he went along.

Before he begins at the bank, however, he makes an important new acquaintance. The purchaser of 'Punishment' turns out to be a man called Jarvis Green, one of the new names in finance. He has spent his youth in Canada and has returned to old England with young money. He is scarcely older than Charlie but already has a large house, 'The Retreat', in Ewell unfortunately, and a reputation for agile enterprise. A poker game takes place at his house every Friday night. He is hospitable but withdrawn. He has a pale face, modern spectacles and receding hair. He looks as worried as an honest man. When Charlie approaches him, about buying 'Punishment', he seems already to know who he is, although he has not yet come into his title. Perhaps Jim Farber has said something. 'Who?' Green says.

The financier (as the newspapers call him) is disinclined to sell the picture, although he has had to go and check that he is indeed the owner. He invites Charlie to the house, however, and acts as though he owes him some debt of gratitude. Charlie asks his advice about joining the Norwegians. 'I think you should, Charlie,' Jarvis says.

Jarvis Green's house is built in glazed brick and has a

green-tile roof. A lot of money has been spent on it; it resembles a road-house of the 'thirties. The bathrooms are identically appointed, though in different shades. The paintings all carry hooded lights. At Christmas, Jarvis Green selects one of them to reproduce and insists, in smallish type, that it comes 'From the collection of Mr and Mrs Jarvis Green'. Charlie is touched by the mild look of puzzlement behind Jarvis's week-end spectacles. Is his fear that the money will never run out and that it will always put upon him this tax of thinking what to do with it? Charlie's connoisseurship is precious to his host and, without profitable motive, they profit from each other's company. While the breakfast-room is being finished at the flat (it takes time to match the gate-legged table exactly), Charlie even comes to stay and travels up to town in Jarvis's other Rolls. Alas, one can no longer park in the West End.

Jarvis is married to an actress whose early parts called on her to unbutton her shirt or to get it wet. Shona is dark, not to say dirty, and her career has lost way, despite the fact that Jarvis once invested a Swiss sum in a vehicle intended to carry her to the stars. Jarvis accepted the loss with good humour but it was not the kind of joke he cared to hear twice. Shona now wears her hair low on her forehead and collects bottles. There is a child, who lacks friends.

Charlie is a success at the bank. He plays Royal Tennis with one of the partners. On the day after Charlie's father dies, the bank is due to give a three-wine lunch for Jarvis Green. Rumour promises that he and the bank are coming to an arrangement. Fred Kirby, the Norwegians' favourite mouthpiece among City Editors, is one of the guests.

Charlie wears a funereal tie, but he goes to the lunch. He has a few drinks first with Pip Lethbridge, in London Wall, and when he looks through the peep-hole of the partners' dining room, he sees that Jarvis is already there. He pushes open the door on its leathern hinges (a silent house tradition) and misses the low step into the room. He stamps out one loud syllable which raises a dozen faces in his direction. 'Good Lordship, it's Charlesworth,' Jarvis Green says.

Fred Kirby makes space for Charlie to sit beside him. Fred has long been Jarvis's loud supporter against the City establishment. Fred's paper is the people's friend and he has encouraged its C 3 readers to back Green's 'big deal for the small man'. Kirby has a good war record (though not in a good regiment) and shrapnel in the right leg. He likes rich company and rich food, but there is some steel in him, and always will be. He has promoted Jarvis not least because he is not a gentleman. It amuses him (and his Canadian proprietor) to see the City yield ground without breaking ranks.

'By the way, Charlie,' Jarvis says, 'I'm most awfully sorry about your father. Presumably all your friends are going to have to start calling you "My Lord" from now on.'

'Not all of them, sir,' Charlie says. 'Just you, Jarvis.'

'Well,' says the Chairman at last, 'I rather think it's time I proposed a small toast.'

Just how close is the relationship to be between the bank and the Jarvis Green Organisation? Fred Kirby notices that the new Lord Marsden drinks without enthusiasm to the liaison. 'I thought you and Jarvis were rather good friends?'

'We are,' Charlie says, 'and here's to him and to my brave employers and their, I hope, long spoons.'

'Spoken like a true friend, old boy, spoken like a true friend.'

'He cheats at cards, you know,' Charlie says, 'not that I blame him.'

'I beg your pardon?'

'Jarvis.'

The Chairman is too far away, and too earnest with enthusiasm, to catch what Charlie is suggesting, but he suspects a curdling in the smooth afternoon and looks sourly at Charlie. Before the party breaks up in time for after hours trading, Fred Kirby is awarded a green folder of facts and figures. He is already fashioning his piece: 'Jarvis Green – that no-nonsense, new-school-tied young man who knows what's what and be damned to who's who – told me that his new fund will give everyone a chance to participate in the exciting industrial and technological prospects. Special situations are Jarvis's speciality. Few people will want to miss being aboard when his gravy train pulls out on Monday morning...' Yet before Kirby limps back to his limousine (as City Editor he has city perks), he makes a date for lunch with Charlie Marsden.

They go to a chophouse, good grills, no women.

'Come on, old boy, what've you got on him?'

'Jarvis? Nothing.'

'You're looking for something to do, I gather.'

'Am I? I've got these acres, you know,' Charlie says.

'What happened at the bank exactly?'

'I left it,' Charlie says. 'Working for people's a pill.'

'You said he cheated at cards.'

'It's rather endearing, don't you think? It's a skill, not a necessity. He doesn't mind losing. He's a very generous chap. However, yes, he does. He wants to see what he can get away with, even though he hasn't got any use for what he gets.'

'So you think he's a wrong 'un, old boy, do you?'

'He's the sort of man your readers want him to be,' Charlie said. 'You should know. After all, you made him up.'

Fred Kirby looked at the old wine through new glasses. ''47's all finished, maestro?'

'You had the last bottle, Mr Kirby.'

'On to the '52s then. There isn't much more to make of him really now, is there? What goes up must come down, old boy. Rule of the road. What's your grudge?'

'I don't have a grudge. I rather like the bastard.'

'There must be some dirt,' Kirby says, 'because there always is, isn't there?'

'Well, man is a dirty beast,' Charlie says.

'So what do you feel about doing this little job for us?'

'I'm not gunning for him, you know, Jarvis.'

'We'll pay by the bushel,' Fred Kirby said. 'I wouldn't curse you with a contract or anything. A gentleman's agreement, what do you say?'

'Who's the other gentleman?' Charlie said, but he shook hands.

The success of 'The Gunroom' encouraged Theo Plant to open two more restaurants: 'The Golden Bowl' and 'The Silver Ditto'. The latter was in Battersea, but Theo's clientèle followed him across the river and 'The Silver Ditto' soon acquired that louche reputation respectable people required for parking in unlikely postal districts. Charlie took the Countess there occasionally. One evening he saw Katya Lowell dining in a red-benched booth with Jarvis Green.

The Countess proved a practised and practising lover. She had her own money and her own place. When tact was required, she knew not to touch. Without expecting constancy, she was constantly available. She educated Charlie to respond to her love, but she never imagined that he would love her. They pretended to a solemnity which was evidence of their facetiousness. They were refined in their foreplay, which always took place after the event. Charlie's appetite for that white, dark-whiskered body was maintained by the subtlety of her service. They were lovers without being in love and passionate without passion. For Charlie, during the months of their affair, there was the chance to elaborate, in private, a style nowhere current in public. They revived a small era, for two. They never discussed marriage; they were too polite.

Charlie had brimmed with desire when he was twenty, but had always spilled it before it could overflow. He had never supposed that sex and love went together. He had never exclusively desired boys; they had been available and he had availed himself. The Countess bore him the particular affection a woman feels for a man whom she has weaned away from his own sex, but the diligence she showed was actually less than Charlie required. The basic equipment was not so very different: meat and fish, 'The Silver Ditto' proved, can take much the same sauce. Even so, the spontaneity with which he fell in love with Katya Lowell that night in S.W.12 did rather surprise him. He had seen her before more than ten years earlier, and she had looked much the same. He had remarked her then and he had continued casually to remark her ever since, but as one might a monument which, to one's mild astonishment, moves from one part of town to another. The Countess observed his new interest. 'Who is she?' she says.

'Don't you know Katya Lowell?'

He discovered that Jarvis Green's Canadian activities had been probably no more unscrupulous than those of any other operator. However, he did gain some unexpectedly choice information about his acquisition of some grain elevators near Montreal. An angry man with a memory and bruises knew his cousin, a lady-in-waiting. Charlie began to compile a dossier on Jarvis, less from animosity than from that curious determination not to be beaten which had led him, in the Bond Street past, to continue bidding for a lot he did not greatly want. He went through old balance sheets and provincial newspapers quite as if he were composing a pointless and punctilious monograph. The secrecy of his labours lent them glamour. The Countess called him naughty for concealing things from her and fondled him for it. She suspected a new boy.

Falling in love with Katya Lowell is something he could have done without. He is eager to see her again not least because he hopes that it will prove to have been a mirage, this sudden embarrassing flower. He rationalises his excitement by arguing to himself that it must be her connection with

Jarvis Green which has excited him. Since Jarvis has no notion that anyone is hunting out his past, Charlie has no difficulty in resuming visits to 'The Retreat', where he enjoys the challenge of detecting the marked cards. A certain affection revives for Jarvis whose grand good fortune has not yet cured him of his hobby. One Friday night Charlie mentions Katya Lowell's name (Shona has retired to count her bottles). How well does Jarvis know her? There is something older about Jarvis now. His hair is thicker, a new shade of luxuriant auburn. He has adopted contact lenses, which darken his eyes. His face still has no lines (people would only read between them) but he has never before shaved so noticeable a beard.

'Katya Lowell?' Jarvis says. 'I like her work. You know that.'

'Do you know her personally at all? What's she like?'

'She's very beautiful. You must have seen her.'

'I'm told she never smiles,' Charlie says. 'Why is that?'

'She smiles,' Jarvis says.

Jarvis was always dangerous, but before he was dangerous with ignorance, which thought things simple. Now he appears more sinister, as if he knew what things were like, and still thought them simple. Is he involved in drugs? Does he buy or does he sell? Shona wears a tiny silver spoon beneath her dry shirt. Cards are now merely sociable. Jarvis goes out in the middle of the game to say 'Yes' to people who have called. He has a butler who bulges. Yet in public he continues to play the benefactor. His stock is high. He is building a home for handicapped children. His own child has lacked friends and is now at a school which has classes of one.

Charlie's dossier grows fat. Is his fascination with Jarvis maintained because Jarvis is a line, however charged, which may lead to Katya Lowell? He is not the only hope. Camilla keeps a busy table. She entertains a lot of foreigners and people; Marcus's firm has taken over a failing French sale room and gallery. *Ça remonte maintenant.* It is easy for the Hickses to invite Katya Lowell, among interesting others.

As soon as Charlie heard that she was coming, he announced to the Countess that their liaison was at an end.

'Oh you are in love,' she said.

'It wouldn't be honourable to continue, Anya. It would be pleasant; it wouldn't be honourable.'

'Is it a woman?'

'It is a woman.'

She kissed him for his fidelity. 'Is she yours?'

'Is she mine?'

'Is she yet yours?'

'I haven't actually spoken to her yet,' Charlie said.

'You *are* in love, my darling. You *are* in love.' The Countess looked out in reproach at the printennial park, as if it had been slyly installed behind her back. She broke open a diamond bracelet on her wrist and held it in her hand, a transplanted peasant weighing produce. 'So... this is not a little premature? What will you do if – things do not happen?'

'I love her,' Charlie said.

'I understand. But this is nice in some ways. We can stay friends?'

'That's exactly it,' Charlie said. 'If we didn't do this now, we never could. I should have to be cruel.'

'And you are not cruel, dear Charles, are you?'

He kissed her hand. She had been his foreign cruise. He had learned much and he was happy to be home. His love was serious; he prepared for it as if for a vocation. He did not desire Katya Lowell; he wanted her. Conquest would not be enough. He intended marriage. He was prepared to be patient and courtly. He would conceal from her only what style deplored. Because he was in no hurry (though he thought of nothing else), he felt neither embarrassment nor timidity when he sat across from her at the Hickses' dinner. He rehearsed no jokes, deployed no winsome solemnities. He

watched her talking prompter's French – a single word
reviving her neighbour's garrulous *analyse* – with the
complaisance of that married man who had sipped whisky, no
water, when she went, challenging and submissive, to listen to
the now transatlantic critic. Now that he was in love, he was
able to look, almost dispassionately, at the object of his
passion, quite as if she were already his long possession. The
first time was an anniversary. The curvature of her nose, its
minute and delicious deviation from the true in both the
vertical and the horizontal axis lent unnerving asymmetry to
those amontillado eyes; their perfection was subtly compro-
mised and hence perfected. The lips were full, not loose. She
never pouted; she was never prim. If she smiled, which Jarvis
said she did, her smile had left no powdered trace. In the
candlelight the butterfly shadows under her cheekbones were
velvet bruises. It was exquisite to love without speech or
introduction. As a boy, he had never imagined love but now,
recreating a spurious childhood of romantic reverie, he would
improvise a long and longing love. She seemed to honour his
invention by the paucity of her own speech. She says only
enough to keep the chatter brilliant among her neighbours.
Her first look at Charlie notices that he notices; the directness
of her glance, intensely feminine, yet sexless in its intensity,
stuns him. There is nothing he would not do; nothing he can.
He is defenceless to the knife that lodges in him; he feels
everything, he feels nothing. Each stage of his love seems so
complete that nothing can be added to it, yet here he is more
helpless, more exalted than ever. How will he get up from the
table? He rises without difficulty. How will he come down?
He comes down beside her on Camilla's fawn leather sofa.

'We have a mutual friend, it seems,' he says.

'You play cards,' she says.

'Yes,' he says, 'what do you do?'

'I paint,' she says.

'With Jarvis.'

'I see him,' she says. 'When I want to.'

'And you want to?'

'You know Jarvis,' she says.

'I know Jarvis,' Charlie says, refusing the brandy, but not the pause the butler brought, 'and I love you.'

'Really?'

'Surely you knew? You are the great and only love of my life.'

'Thank you,' she says.

'I expected you to know. From dinner.'

'I've seen you before,' she says.

'I should like to marry you. This isn't a casual thing. It isn't a modern thing. It's eternal. I love you and I always shall. I realise this may upset your immediate social arrangements and I don't expect an immediate response, but ideally I should like to marry you tomorrow. Or tonight. I should like to catch a steamer and marry you when we reach the open seas. I believe one can still do that.'

'I'm so sorry,' she says, as if he were mortally ill.

'No, no,' he says, 'no, no. Don't look away. This isn't something I shall brandish like a writ. My offer of marriage is now assumed between us, and for ever. I mean it, totally. My love is quite unconditional. I shan't restate it, except on invitation, but a love like mine won't be repeated. It's unique. You are the only woman I shall ever love. Thank you for not smiling.' He makes this speech with a sort of casual humour, as if offering a cigarette, or a city, to someone he suspects does not smoke, or travel. A proposal which might have capped a long courtship becomes its prelude. There is nothing concealed between them, no threat, no trap; he has disclosed his hand by offering it. When he looks at the flat, steel ring on her finger it is as if his glance can make it golden; if she says 'Yes,' it will.

She proves more accessible than Camilla forecast. Charlie ceases to confide in his sister as he and Katya Lowell begin to meet more frequently. Camilla might almost be a rival, lacking the Countess's cosmopolitan code. Charlie is polite; he is unusually polite – 'Look at Charlie's flowers!' – but he is preparing to remove himself from the world of the Hickses. He and Katya will probably live abroad, though he does not fail to notice her attachment to London; the ticking taxis she likes to have waiting at restaurant doors, the underground into which, with a girlish wave, she dives like a brave or drunken guest into an unheated pool. She carries an aura of luxury, but she luxuriates in the mundane. She will wear a model coat one day – and hand-made shoes – and the next she will be in a duffle and scuffed boots. She has a character independent of fashionable consistency. Charlie loves her for the care which she encourages him, without overt encouragement, to lavish on her. She bicycles over to take a hire car to new places he has scouted. They never go to any of Theo Plant's restaurants. Charlie makes an unspoken case against all that they have known before, though he never spoils things with sarcasm or jealousy. When she is not free, he shows no sign of disappointment. He is chaste, even when he is alone; he is waiting for her, even when they are together. Does she suspect that sometime after this meal or that excursion he will try the typical touch: the hand, the kiss, the breast? He remains passionately correct; cadged compensations mean nothing to him. 'You must have had a lot of women,' she says.

'I've had one,' he answers, truth clowning a tactful lie.

And what of Katya Lowell? It is of no moment to Charlie if she is a virgin or a whore. He loves her. The intensity of his feelings does not interrupt his investigations into Jarvis Green. Any man, he comes to realise, as the spoil heap grows, sufficiently researched will yield a criminal, a lunatic or a fool. The more he studies Jarvis the less specific he seems. The dossier fattens but the man grows thinner, until he might be anybody, this wartime refugee from Birmingham parents, the Canadian schoolboy, the teenage victim of a stadium proprietor with carnal designs. The more he discovers the less printable use it seems to Fred Kirby, for if every dull and terrible truth were to be told, everyone would be condemned, which is why such truths are never printed. There is something wonderful in the detail available, if one searches, in a life lacking in all charm or distinction. Jarvis Green is a cheap fiction, a *collage* of incidents from commonplace sources. The history of Jarvis Green is so in tune with the times that one cannot shout it above the hum of the chorusing crowd. Fred Kirby seems to be doling out money for copy bound to go on the spike. Then, one night, Charlie meets Katya Lowell and knows she has been hurt.

She pins his unboxed, leopard-spotted orchid on her lapel and its greenhouse bruises seem allusions to her own.

'How did it happen? It wasn't an accident.'

She smiles. She smiles! 'No,' she says, 'it wasn't. I would have said to anyone else that it was, but not to you, not any more, dear Charles. I want to marry you.'

He gives the waiter the impression that he is anxious to order. The climax of his hopes compels him to give no vulgar sign of it. He has always meant to marry her (his love spreads backward now to give purpose to the moment of his birth, since he was born for this) and now she has come to him. He will neither grab nor exult. He is a lord. Is it unfashionable? Then it pleases him to honour what others find outmoded. In a world where nothing noble is allowed, all nobility becomes the dandy's choice. His lordship takes her lean hand and kisses it. From his pocket he produces a jeweller's box, amateur magician with a single trick. 'I love you,' he says. 'Do I know your parents?'

'I have no parents,' she says. 'I have no one.'

'You have me.'

'This is very beautiful.'

'I had it made. I approve of patronage, don't you?'

'Decidedly,' she says, 'since I approve of you, dear Charles.'

'Shall I kill him for you?'

'I want to marry you,' she says. 'Forget the rest.'

'Both can be managed. I'm perfectly serious.'

'I know that, good Charlie; that's why I am. You mustn't kill anybody.'

'Whoever it is,' he says, 'it can be managed. I can always take my time.'

'Do you love me less because of it?' She holds his hand and forbids it to be a fist.

'Love you less? I told you: my love is infinite; it can never be less, or more. Did they die, your parents?'

'Yes, of course. They'd be alive otherwise, wouldn't they? Don't imagine me an angel, will you?'

'Have no fear. I don't *imagine* you at all. To me you are the only reality. I accept you totally, which is something quite different from imagination. Is it a man?'

'Naturally,' she says. 'But please... I promise you, it's immaterial.'

'Venice, India, Granada, Borneo, where?'

'Venice,' she says, 'but not yet – when it's cold and out of season and we can hear the wind blowing old stories in off the lagoon.'

'And I can finish my Armenian dictionary,' Charlie says.

Jarvis Green keeps a flat, Charlie hears, in Pimlico. Mr Aplin, a private detective, watches it for Charlie, account to the City Editor. His next badly typed log reveals that a woman arrived recently (date appended) and left, after dark, in sunglasses. Charlie has been making some inquiries about steamers. He hopes to be married aboard, without fuss or guests, and to spend at least some months away from England. He speaks once of not returning at all, but Katya nods and kisses him at this and he knows that she does not wish it. The plans for their departure are confirmed. They book on a Greek ship whose Captain can perform the necessary rites. Katya and Charlie buy luggage, then she leaves him, in a cab, for the last time, perhaps. The report of the private detective discloses that a woman goes that night to Westmoreland Street and that she is wearing a model coat, scuffed boots. When Katya and Charlie meet again he looks at her, not with suspicion or fear or jealousy, but with attention. They are not yet lovers; he has never touched her body or even seen it. They do not swim or bathe together. She is always dressed.

He neither hates nor despises her. The information of Mr Aplin counts against Jarvis; it has nothing to do with her.

They sail on the *Elene* from Tilbury. The gods give them rain and a taxi and a Greek primed to carry the luggage up the ridged plank under a snappy awning. The dossier is ready for Fred Kirby. A more cunning man than Charlie might have made dispositions to secure a fortune when the first articles appear and the City bears start to bait their prey. Can anything save Jarvis once the lawyers sign the warrant: publish and he's damned? Fred's proprietor, however, does not want to give the green light too fast; he prefers to flash an unobtrusive amber to warn some at least of the paper's readers. To this end, sly emphasis is given in the gossip columns to Jarvis's private life, his absences on sunny islands when decisions are taken: up to his neck in the Caribbean, how cool can a tycoon be? The chart of Jarvis Green Securities dips; a reverse head and shoulders makes its downward prognosis. Pip Lethbridge asks Charlie what he knows. Charlie says that he cannot say that he knows anything. 'In that case, one's safe obviously to stay in,' says Pip, and gets out.

Charlie cares only for the moment when he and Katya Lowell will be together in front of the Captain. Yet, like a dreamer who tells the truth even though he recognises the court is made of playing cards, honour requires him to ask Kirby to withhold publication until his return from Venice. (It smacks of cowardice to cut a man down *in absentia*.)

Captain Panselinos affects surprise, first at the request and then at the money, but Katya becomes Lady Marsden in the Bay of Biscay. Steel turns to gold. Not until they return to their cabin does Charlie see his wife's nakedness, and the marks upon it. She studies his face for contempt or horror. She sees neither. Marriage does not alter the rhythm of his tact. It is no crude green signal for him. He lends it a meaning beyond possession or permission, beyond all present devaluations. What is laughable to others does not make him smile; because others laugh, he does not. 'I want to kill him,' he says. 'I'll tell them not to publish; I'll kill him instead.'

'Charles, please, do neither,' she says.

Though Katya has been to his flat several times, she has never remarked the coincidence between its décor and the paintings in her show at the Farber Gallery. She walks through her own creation without recognising it; her art is beautiful but her beauty does not respond to it. All right, he will love her for her indifference to his compliment. There can be no question of their living in the flat (since it is a joke she does not choose to see), so he commissions the young estate agent (now on his own, Peter Bent, in Clarges Street) to sell it for him during his absence. 'Are you not getting married, my lord, after all?'

'Of course,' Charlie said.

They go ashore at Venice under veils of rain, as if fugitives from some scandal so divine that they can be lent the weather to dress their incognito. The lagoon is thin of colour; Katya might have mixed its washiness from the cleaning spirit in a blue glass. Most of the tourist shops are closed. They seek deserted places, distant *fondamenta*. They find a boatman, mantled in a glistening cowl, whose French polished cabin can be theirs for the month. He is surly and Charlie disdains to tip him in advance to procure his geniality. Only on the last day, out in the staked lagoon, does Charlie give him what might have made him sing. He shows no gratitude. He is a man of character. They like him better for his unsold expression and that evening, lying in a broad and canopied bed, under plaster rosettes, they are willing to believe that here and there they will find more such alien beings to furnish and not intrude upon their seclusion. Charlie has what he wants; dream and reality march in step. But Venice is at once perfect and imperfect; Katya is loyal and loving, but she cannot lie and Charlie loves her too much to connive at pretty pretence. She reminds him of that letter from Albertine in which the girl agrees to accompany Proust's narrator to Venice, a letter which comes when she is already dead. 'I've always known,' she says. 'I always knew that I would meet someone that deserved my love and to whom I would want to give it and it would be too late.'

'It's not too late,' he says.

'Oh Charlie, my lord, my lord!'

'Nothing can prevent me giving you what you want. I love you too much.'

'That's it,' she says. They are on the Giudecca; the paling sea jostles over the settled granite of the jetty, transparent as lace on a Flemish wrist. A bridge takes a high step over the narrow canal and they stand up there, isolated captains on a stone ship, as the waves cuff and spread along the quay. She turns to him with tears running uneven along the uneven nose. He kisses salt. 'You love me,' she says, 'and that is why... it's no good.' She shrugs and turns her face upwards so that rain dilutes the tears; particular and elemental blend. 'I must go back to England,' she says.

'We'll go anywhere you want to go,' he says. 'You doubt love's range; I don't.'

'Charlie,' she says, 'I love you. Don't weaken now. I love you. Nothing that happens in the world can ever affect that. People might say that I recognise in you only what reflects my own self. It's not true. I recognise your love, and that's not the same at all. Don't doubt my love, but I've been what I am for as long as I've been alive, just as you say you loved me before you even met me. I was what I am from before I knew it, let alone you. I never met anyone whose love I trusted and believed before. I saw it in you like a gift that no one could refuse, a kind of talent. I honour it, Charlie. Oh and by the way, I've always dreamed of titles, of election, of a special world. You and I and our boatman...!' She smiled lovely pain.

'Who began it? That man at the party, the one who was killed?'

'Harry? I can't make him the scapegoat. I wanted it, Charlie. I escaped and I couldn't endure it. My parents died and I escaped, how could I go unscathed? Unpunished?'

'You have me,' he said. 'I haven't escaped.'

'And then I began to sell,' she said.

The clouds shuffled the scenery above their heads, parting to show ragged blue wounds that closed again, stitched with the warm rain. A black-cloaked woman in another story went along a wall with a canvas-capped basket. 'Perhaps I killed him,' Charlie said, 'Groves. I'll certainly kill the others.'

'Which would only make me deserve it more,' she says. 'You're too intelligent not to know that. We can't run and we can't destroy what pursues us. Hurt him, you destroy us. Don't let them print what you've written.'

'It's almost out of my hands.'

'Burn it, Charlie. Unless you're willing to play his part.'

'The only thing in the world I can't do is not love you,' he says. 'Be cold.'

'Ah, there we are then, aren't we? I'd die with you, Charlie. We can take the ship back and at night there's always the rail and the sea...'

'Blasphemy. I married beauty and beauty must live,' Charlie says. 'And I want to live with it.'

She turns and kisses him, the rain gushing over their gargoyle faces. They hold the kiss as if some cruel director refused to cry 'cut'. They go back at last to the ferry stage bludgeoned with water that swells their coats. They are lumbered like the wood of a dishonest woodman who sells it wet, by weight. They steam in the warm lobby of the palazzo and accept amazed attention. ('What were you *doing,* Contessa?') At dinner they mourn, delicious together under the candelabra, and the waiters bless them with happiness. That night Charlie is pierced by her coarse cry and cries himself, knowing that she is artist enough even to manage a perfect fake. 'No,' he says. 'I'll have them burn the stuff. I haven't had the money and besides, the best parts are at my bank. Perhaps I always knew.'

'Oh Charles, you'll hate me in the end.'

'No,' he says. 'I shall never hate you and I can never take his place because of it. Perhaps it will pass one day and we shall be alone again.' As they spoke, they were placed by the cruel director in sight of the corner of the Doge's palace, where Adam and Eve are rubbed by the chemical wind.

They return to London. Charlie calls Jarvis Green and arranges, in return for the destruction of the dossier, that his wife will see her cruel lover whenever she wants to or whenever he summons her, which is the same thing. Charlie dines on those occasions with Marcus and Camilla and company. It is generally agreed that he and his wife are ideally happy. Jarvis Green's shares recover. He and the Norwegians are successfully married. This year his Christmas card reproduces 'Punishment', by Katya Lowell.

Oxbridge Blues

No one ever accused the Geary brothers of being alike. It was true that both had blue eyes, but then Victor was dark and Philip was fair. Victor was always said to be going places; Pip to be doing quite well considering. Their parents, sensitive to the strain on Pip's psyche, sent him to a less demanding school than his brother. He scraped into Selwyn, while Victor was a scholar at King's. If Pip had any consolation, it was that he was both bigger and stronger than his older brother. Yet it was typical that Pip should just miss his Blue (an American Olympic oarsman came into the reckoning at the last minute), whereas Victor had been President of Shooting and, without raising a sweat, was elected to the Hawks' Club, thus becoming eligible for an enviable tie. Pip smiled at the news; Victor frowned. 'These things don't matter any more,' he said. Good luck weighed more heavily on Victor than bad on his junior.

Good old Pip drank a lot of beer with the boys and was always free for a frame of snooker. Victor preferred wine, if it was worth drinking, and was usually at the library. Pip reckoned he did bloody well to get a Third in Geography, two summers after Victor had walked away with a starred First in Economics. Pip's sporting connections secured him a job with a travel agency, after a score of sorry interviews for more promising prospects. Victor had already passed top into the Treasury. He was soon walking to lunch at the Reform, often parading across the park in the company of an assistant-secretary. They swung their umbrellas in unison, bowlers tilted slightly forward, like civilised Guards' officers. Pip commuted daily to Bishopsgate from Hatfield Peverel, where he lived with his parents.

Victor was not only cleverer than his brother (and than most people), he was also better looking. Wine put on less weight than beer, but he had a fineness of feature – high cheek-bones, white skin, keen brows – and an accurately hawkish air: he never had to pounce more than once. Philip had a broad nose, as if he had fought for some boxing title, and lost; his jaw had the beefiness to be seen in thick Roman copies of Greek originals. Victor's brilliance was made flesh in the intensity of his gaze and the elegance of his long, white hands. He frightened a lot of women, but usually they contrived to be frightened in his direction. It was no great surprise when he acquired Wendy de Souza, or she him. Each took the other as a kind of prize to which no one else could possibly be entitled.

Wendy was the star of her Oxford year. She acted famously for O.U.D.S. and a gushing reviewer said that she was the only girl in Oxford who managed to be naked with all her clothes on: she had one of those mouths and two of those eyes. Her poetry appeared in *Poetry* and some of it was in French. She knew words like *couillons*. An Earl (admittedly Irish) at Brasenose was reputed to have offered her acres for a single kiss. ('Where exactly?' said a jealous theatrical. 'The kiss or the acres?' said another.) Someone wanted to know if it was true that she had been born in Alexandria. 'Someone has to be,' she said, in that Fortnum's accent of hers, and quoted Cavafy, the bitch.

Her worst enemies admired her. She was expected to go straight into starring roles in the West End. (Her décolleté reading of Goneril had brought producers down from London.) Instead, after a single meeting in the rooms of a pear-shaped, matchmaking Head of House, she decided that she would marry Victor Geary. 'He is the man of my life,' she declared. 'That pale face is my fortune, and don't bother to point out the misquotation.'

What did it matter that she failed, surprisingly, to get a First? Victor had enough academic distinctions for both of them; her beauty made nonsense of mundane rankings. The wedding was reported in all the papers as the smartest of the year. It took place in the chapel of the college where they had met. All the foreseeable Cabinet Ministers, Heads of Legation, Judges, Nobel Prizemen and Regius Professors from the two great universities were among the congregation. How could some sub-editor fail to put the caption 'Oxbridge Blues' under the photograph of the smiling couple? (Actually Victor was frowning, but no one looked at him when Wendy was on his arm.)

Nothing distinct was said in the society magazines about either set of parents. Victor's father was, in fact, the Essex branch manager of an insurance company; Wendy's was a wholesaler of oriental and Middle Eastern food. Neither was anything to be ashamed about, but in any event beauty and brains provided their own pedigree.

They went to live in a narrow terrace house in Canonbury. (Doors were only just beginning to turn primrose yellow in the borough.) Mr de Souza helped with the deposit. Victor's Treasury position was impressive but his stipend was not. He supplemented it with articles for journals with very long paragraphs, either anonymously or under a pseudonym. (Though he never smiled about it, he was often in the amusing position of annotating his own cuttings, sometimes cuttingly, before passing them to the mandarins.) Wendy was soon preparing a series of broadcasts of European poetry; she read a number of the selections herself in that husky voice of hers. She and Victor continued to see their Oxbridge friends, most of whom had married each other. The first pregnancies were reported, and the first separations.

Pip was still travelling up and down from Essex, the

bachelor. He seemed happy to plan world-wide itineraries for bankers and Caribbean holidays for the classier sort of share-pusher. He learned tactfully to distinguish between what a man was prepared to spend on the firm and what was available for the wife and kids. As time went on, he grew fluently cosmopolitan: he seemed to have been everywhere. 'How did you find the Carlyle, sir?' he would ask, and, 'Was I right about the *pistes* at Méribel?' Who would guess that he had never left England except to play club soccer in Knokke-le-Zoute? He got a discount for Victor and Wendy when they went to Turkey, but they both contracted enteritis in Ismir, while looking for Seferis's birthplace, and their thanks were shaded. Pip took holidays with his parents in the Lake District, which his mother remembered from her childhood. Victor and Wendy could not imagine how he could endure the life he led. All he did was to read cheap thrillers and play soccer with this team of clerks and workers from a local jam factory, watch dreadful television (he would quote the commercials) and dig his parents' garden. Presumably there were girls, but it all seemed hopelessly provincial. How could he be so happy? Victor frowned when he thought about Pip, but then he frowned when he thought about most things. Wendy was always asking him what was wrong. 'Nothing,' he told her.

One day, soon after his twenty-ninth birthday, Pip rang Victor to announce that he was engaged to be married. 'Anyone I know?' asked his brother, who was waiting for a call from the Chief Secretary, to whom he had forwarded a rather sly minute.

'Most improbable,' said Pip. 'She's a girl called Maxine. I call her Max.'

'Wait a minute,' Victor said, 'I just want to be sure that there isn't anybody on the line. Did you hear a sort of click just now?'

'I thought it was you, mate, disapproving.'

'Don't be silly. What is there to disapprove of? Marriage is an honourable estate.'

'She's scared stiff of you,' Pip said. 'You will be nice to her, won't you?'

'I'm nice to everybody,' Victor said. 'Where did you meet?'

'At a local hop,' Pip said. 'The Rotary have an annual do in Chelmsford. I don't know if you remember the Dimmages, used to live along the Maldon Road?'

'It is rather a long time ago,' Victor said.

'Oh I know, there've been fifty budgets since then, haven't there?'

'What sort of girl is she?'

'She didn't go to university, if that's what you mean,' Pip said.

'That isn't what I meant at all. Millions of people didn't go to university.'

'Yes, but you don't know many of them, do you? She helps a vet at the moment. She's the Dimmages' niece. She's only twenty-two. I think she's rather bright. I know what you're thinking,. what would I know about bright?'

'She sounds like just the girl we need,' Victor said. 'Frenchie's developed a bit of a lump in one of her tits. Do you think she'd take a look at it?'

'At the usual rates, I'm sure she'd be delighted, old son.'

'You'd better bring her to dinner. I'll have a word to Wendy and see when's the best day.'

'Preferably one when you haven't got eight professors and the man who's made the big breakthrough in astrophysics, if it's all the same to you.'

'We know very few astrophysicists,' Victor said. 'Would you rather it was just the four of us?'

'Max isn't a fool or anything, Vic – '

'*Please* don't call me Vic; I hate being confused with a cough cure.'

'Aye there's the rub!' Pip said. 'It's simply that she's never been exposed to the full Oxbridge artillery. Any day next week, except Thursday. Thursday we're going to see her parents, in Mitcham. Tell me, how are things with you at the moment? I gather they're a bit sticky.'

'You have the advantage of me,' Victor said.

'I only wish I could serve an ace, then! I meant this credit squeeze and the balance of payments. If you make the travel allowance much smaller, I shall have to go out and work for a living. I wouldn't like to have your job at this stage.'

'No, well, you're not likely to get it, are you?'

'Any day except Thursday,' said Pip.

Victor frowned and replaced the receiver. He lived in a state of agonised complacency. He had nothing to worry about, and it worried him. He was well thought of by his superiors and he was too firmly on the ladder ever to have to bother about the snakes. His wife was not only enviably beautiful, she was also loyal and good-natured. How could he complain if, having married a girl from whom he might have expected a life of testing anguish, he found himself with a grocer's daughter who was always there with a smile and a hot meal when he got home from Whitehall? He could hardly reproach her for wanting to give up an arid job at Broadcasting House in order to look after the house or for her adorable hints that she longed to have a child. Why was he secretly so appalled by the peace of mind to which he was treated? When the first of their friends broke up, or divorced, he wondered what curious immaturity rendered Wendy so banal. He had married Goneril and here was Cordelia. She had even turned down a chance to do Baudelaire in the *Critical Studies Series*. She bought women's magazines. She said she liked the pictures of babies.

Maxine would have to turn out to be pregnant, of course. Her puffy complexion showed it more than her body: motherhood had struck her a blow across the face. Her hair had been elaborately done, in metallic ringlets, as if to distract the eye from the rounding parcel in her lap, but the colour was so brazen that one looked instantly downwards. Victor and Wendy were used to discussing sex in recently liberated terms with their Oxbridge friends, but Maxine's condition, and her rural provenance, put an embargo on Canonbury frankness. Even Frenchie's lump (benign, nothing to worry about, honest) proved more an embarrassment than a source of conversation. It was left to Pip to mention the forthcoming baby, after a spoon-clicking soup course, and so deliver the evening from silence. He seemed more loudly contented than ever. He told City jokes and made Wendy laugh her candid, ringing laugh. Maxine's eyes rolled anxiously in her head, as she observed her host's thin humour. When she had wiped her lips ('Ever such good chicken'), she asked earnestly about Wendy's work; she only wished she had the qualifications for doing something brilliant.

'I only do it for the money,' Wendy said, 'don't I, darling?'

'Of course not,' Victor said, opening the reserve bottle of plonk. Pip could certainly put it away.

'This is ever such a nice house,' Maxine said.

'We got it when it was young,' Victor said. 'Where are you thinking of living yourselves?'

'There's a cottage just down the road from Mum and Dad,' Pip said. 'Where the Red Indians used to live, if you remember.'

'Red Indians?' Wendy covered her mouth. She could see from Victor's frown that she had better not laugh. 'Whatever do you mean, Pip, Red Indians?'

'People called Wigg,' Pip said. 'Hence wigwam, hence Navajo, hence Red Indian. We used to go and wah-wah-wah until they came out. Remember, Vic?'

'Not really. You're seriously going to go on commuting? You must be mad.'

'I'm not too serious about it,' Pip said. 'I've got chums on the train who bag me a beer. I do my neighbour's quick crossword over one shoulder and I cop a quick read of the juicier bits of *Woman's Own* over the other, not to mention a spot of crafty legmanship with the pick of the typing pool across the aisle. The time passes.'

'What about your writing, Pip? You haven't mentioned that.'

'Not in this house,' Pip said.

'*Writing?*'

'It's not what *you'd* call writing,' Pip said, 'but yes. Only to amuse myself, you know. I used to read a lot of these trashy thrillers, but now they've got tables in the trains, some of them, so I thought I'd try my hand.'

'I'd like to see one of them,' Wendy said.

'Oh come on, Wendy, wait till I start writing them in French, then perhaps...'

'Have you shown them to a publisher or anyone?'

'Of course not. It's just to pass the time.'

'What're they about?' Wendy said.

'Sort of down-market James Bond,' Pip said. 'Nothing you could possibly be interested in.'

'I've never understood James Bond,' Victor said.

'He does use some long words, doesn't he?' Maxine said.

The wedding took place in Hatfield Peverel. The company was not glittering. The soccer club was there, and relatives whom Victor had forgotten. A couple of beery chums of Pip's from the Goldie boat of 1958 were the only university representatives. Victor apologised to Wendy for dragging her to so dismal an affair. 'Oh, I enjoyed it,' she said. 'Didn't you think Pip made a good speech?'

'Just the sort of thing to turn the wheels of the Rotary Club,' Victor said.

'Did you know that Maxine did A-level French and History? She got B's in both. And an A in Art.'

'Very impressive,' Victor said.

'I do envy her the baby,' Wendy said.

'We can't afford it,' Victor said. 'We really can't.'

'Why can they?'

'It was an accident,' he said.

'I wish I could have one of those,' she said.

There was a mini-budget that November and a maxi-budget in the spring, followed by another mini-mini-budget in the summer, when the pound came under renewed pressure, and Victor with it. He tired but he never flagged. The birth of Sandra Jane was quickly followed by Maxine's next pregnancy: Dominic. The name struck Victor as pretentious, though he sent floral congratulations which proved more expensive than he had expected. Damned inflation! Wendy's desire for a child seemed more and more bloody-minded. Victor asked whether she would like him to resign from the Treasury and take a job in commerce. 'Can you get one?' she said. It was Maxine who telephoned with the news of the last straw. 'You'll never guess what, Victor. I had to tell you. Pip's had his book accepted.'

'*Book?*'

'One of his thrillers. It's been accepted. It's going to be published.'

'A common consequence of acceptance,' Victor said.

'Sorry?'

'There's no need to apologise. Who's doing it?'

'It's going straight into paperback,' Maxine said. 'They're rushing it out apparently.'

'That's very nice news. What's it called?'

'I don't think you'll like the title very much. It's called *A Bit of Spare*.'

'Sounds just my sort of thing,' Victor said.

'Pip wanted to call it *Randy Rides Again*.'

'Presumably that was rather too up-market,' Victor said.

'He's invented this character called Randy O'Toole. Do you think he ought to change it?'

'He isn't publishing this thing under his own name, is he?' Victor said.

'Why not? It's not as if he's got a reputation to lose or anything, is it?' she said.

'I wasn't thinking of him,' Victor said. 'When is this volume due to appear?'

'Any day. They want to get the second one on the stalls by Christmas.'

'The second one? How many are there?'

'Oh hundreds,' Maxine said. 'Pip reckons he's got at least fifteen ready to be typed and he says he can do them at the rate of about one every ten days. I expect he'll have to use a few whatdoyoucall'ems, don't you, so's not to saturate the market?'

'Pseudonyms,' Victor said. 'I must say one hopes so.'

'I just thought you'd like to know. Give my love to Wendy, won't you? I listened to her on Friday, talking about that Greek poet. It was ever so interesting, tell her.'

'I'm sure she'll be delighted,' Victor said.

A Bit of Spare was not reviewed in *The Times Literary Supplement*. It was not reviewed anywhere. It did not need to be. The first printing was 30,000 and it was soon supplemented. Victor bought a copy at St James's Park station, thrusting it hotly into his briefcase as he saw one of his principals approaching. He read it on a bench in the park during his lunch interval. It was quite as horrifying as he feared. Randy O'Toole made James Bond seem like a character in Henry James. The globe-trotting narrative was littered with spreadeagled corpses and flimsy French underwear. Breasts thrust, nipples stiffened and thighs flashed. Hoarse cries burst forth and moans of rapture escaped. Hardware crackled and knuckle sandwiches wiped the grins off swarthy faces. Gore spurted and limbs snapped like tinder. Randy was a lean package of irresistible virility. Legs parted before him like the Red Sea. At the climax of the book, he managed to get the villain smack between the eyes with a .38 just as he was provoking a screech of rapture from a previously frigid albino Venus, firing simultaneously from both barrels. Victor Geary closed the book with disgust and an intolerable awareness in his, what was the phrase? – mounting manhood – that his brother was not only a cheap disgrace, but the stuff of which best sellers were made.

Randy on the Job followed soon afterwards. Pip's travel agency, of which he was now a partner, promoted a tie-up with the publishers. Tours were arranged to 'Randy Rendezvous'. Victor was so humiliated that he considered applying for a transfer to the Foreign Office, with a view to some distant posting. The randy jests of his colleagues failed to entertain him. He walked past the Smith's at St James's Park – 'The New Philip Geary Is Here!' – with averted eyes. He tried to believe that the nightmare would pass. It persisted. Pip's imagination was evidently as boundless as it was crude. A female agent called 'Darling' made her unsubtle appearance. When Pip revealed that he had bought a Rolls-Royce Silver Cloud, Victor minuted that the tax levels on the upper income brackets ought perhaps to be looked at again. Wendy wanted to know when she could go for a ride in the new car.

'You can't be serious,' Victor said.

'Not all the time, no,' Wendy said. 'Hence...'

'I don't in the least grudge Pip the money,' Victor said, 'but I do think he might have contrived a way to get rich without quite such a consummate display of totally farmyard mentality. One would never think he'd been to Cambridge.'

'It doesn't do anybody any harm,' Wendy said, 'when you come to think about it.'

'When you come to think about it,' Victor said, 'you'll realise the utter *scandal* of an intelligent person uttering that sort of shallow nonsense. I don't say that Pip's books ought to be banned, but no one, surely, could argue that they shouldn't be burned. That kind of muck acts on the body politic like – oh like a spoonful of sugar in a diabetic's coffee. God almighty, Wendy, why go to university if you can't show some

sense of discrimination. He's welcome to the money, but
really – '

'They want us to go with them to the Aegean in June,'
Wendy said. 'Maxine called. They're hiring a yacht and they
want us to go with them.'

'I can't afford that sort of thing,' Victor said.

'Pip's treat. They insist.'

'I can't afford the time,' Victor said. 'It looks as if there may
be a policy U-turn with a view to a spring election and I shall
have to be in London. Don't tell anyone, of course.'

'Everyone's guessed already,' Wendy said. 'A holiday
wouldn't hurt us, for once.'

'If you really want to swan around the Aegean in a yacht on
the proceeds of Pip's disgusting rubbish, we'd better do it, I
suppose.'

'That's settled then,' Wendy said.

'Presumably Dominic and Sandra and the new one, what's
it called – '

'Justin.'

'Presumably you're prepared to endure their endless row,
for the pleasure of water-skiing in front of coachloads of
gawking Germans.'

'Any day,' Wendy said.

The yacht was bigger than even Victor had expected. The
children had their own quarters and their new Norland
nanny. Also on board was a film producer called 'Curly'
Bonaventura, who had bought the six-figure rights to *Randy
Rides Again* (of course the title was too good not to be used in
the end) and he had options on the rest of the series. He was
also 'actively planning' a film of *Darling Does It*, if he could
find the right girl. Bonaventura seemed the very type of the
bone-headed Hollywood producer and his wife was a bottle-
fed blonde. He called Pip a genius and said that he would do
anything for him. Victor had to qualify his contempt when he
discovered that 'Curly' had won the top prize for Latin verse

composition in Italy in 1938 and was a certified marine engineer. As for Carlotta, she had studied the cello under Casals and played so beautifully one evening when they were anchored off Santorini that it brought tears to the eyes, dammit.

The weather was perfect; the *meltemmi* held off, the sea was calm. There was just enough breeze for them to be able to sail without the engine. The cook was excellent, the captain accommodating. They put in at the small islands like Folegandros and Anafi. Pip was enraptured. He went looking at houses. What could be more delightful than to own a little beach and a shack nearby? They were giving them away, if you had the money. Victor frowned at a Greek newspaper. Only the long words made sense to him and Wendy was too busy having a good time to help him with the short ones. 'Curly' was always available to take her water-skiing. She was over thirty, but no one would have thought so. Maxine was quite the matron by comparison. She came and leaned on the railing next to where Victor was looking pessimistic about trends, a paper-clip in his mouth. 'You ought to try it,' she said, 'water-skiing. You've got the figure. Pippy's much too thick around the middle, but you've kept your figure brilliantly.'

'All that sitting around I do,' he said.

'You do make me laugh,' she said. 'What about this sun?'

'Yes indeed,' Victor said, as the breeze rattled the flimsies.

'You're quite right,' she said, 'it's all a bit of an outrage really, living like the idle rich, lazing about like this, all these meals and things prepared for us.'

'It is the business of the wealthy man/To give employment to the artisan,' Victor said.

'Who is that?' Maxine said. 'It's not Chesterton, is it?'

'Belloc,' Victor said. 'You were close.'

'I wish I'd been educated properly,' Maxine said. 'The thing I really envy about you, Vic, is, you've got inner resources. I wish I had inner resources.'

'I don't imagine you're ever likely to need them, are you, Max, now?'

'Don't be too sure,' she said. 'Haven't you ever read Greek tragedy?'

'In my day,' he said, 'I was known to. Why?'

'Because people do have falls, don't they? I've been catching up in a Penguin. You can have too much and then suddenly you don't have anything at all. It can happen, can't it?'

'Not if you have Curly's accountant. Though of course it may entail living in the Bahamas or somewhere penitential like that. I trust Pip doesn't have to be on the train from Hatfield Peverel every day in order to maintain his inspiration, because that could become a bit prohibitive at current rates.'

'He's got these two electric typewriters,' Maxine said. 'One for Randy and one for Darling. We may have to go to Hollywood soon actually, because Curly wants him out there for the casting and stuff. Pip wants to take a house on the beach.'

'That sounds rather exciting,' Victor said.

'If that's the sort of thing that excites you,' Maxine said.

'I was thinking of you. You're looking very California at the moment, I must say.'

'Mothers of three shouldn't wear bikinis, in other words!' Maxine said. 'Wendy's really beautiful, isn't she? Curly can't take his eyes off her. I must say I fancy a swim, don't you, before the next dose of vine leaves and things? Coming?'

She waited while Victor locked his papers in the cabin. Randy O'Toole had made him security-conscious. They passed Curly and Wendy on the gangway. Wendy's body was almost black with the sun; her teeth gleamed at a joke that Bonaventura was telling, in Italian. Victor's holiday had interrupted a crash course in the language (*anticipando* the Common Market), but he failed to appreciate the punch line which the producer signalled by putting an arm round Wendy's shoulders and squeezing her to him. 'Ciao, Victor.'

They swam to a small beach, from which they could just see the others having drinks on the after-deck of the yacht, under the laced awning. 'I say,' Maxine said, 'I'm going to take my things off, do you mind?'

'I don't mind a bit,' Victor said. 'After all, nakedness began in Greece.'

'I'd never have done it once,' she said, 'but I think it's the money. I don't care what I do any more. It's ever so much nicer, I find. Why don't you do the same?'

'I might well,' he said, 'but you go on.'

'You didn't think much of me, Vic, did you, when you first saw me?'

'I reserved my position,' he said.

'You are a scream sometimes, honestly,' she said. 'Reserved my position! That's one way of describing it, I suppose.'

'Describing what?'

'You keep such a straight face,' she said, 'I can't help laughing.'

'I wish I knew something about music,' Victor said, kicking off his trunks.

'That's better,' she said, 'isn't it? Just as long as Nanny doesn't see us.'

'Do you think she'd send us to bed without any supper?' Victor said.

'I imagine that would be the last place,' Maxine said. 'Why don't you take a course? In music. It's never too late.'

'I don't think I could endure to be a beginner,' he said.

'You only live once,' Maxine said.

'It is a comfort, isn't it?' Victor said.

They could hear Maxine's laugh even on the boat, where Wendy was sipping a daiquiri, legs stretched to the last of the red-faced sun as she listened to Curly's account of a snowball party he had given in Beverly Hills with the temperature in the high seventies. Carlotta watched as Curly showed Wendy how he had inserted a snowball in the front of a stuffy starlet's dress. Pip saw what people meant about that mouth and those eyes.

Maxine and Victor swam slowly back to the boat. The murmur of their voices promised that they had found something serious to talk about. When they had hauled themselves aboard, they stood dripping, at the far end of the deck, and finished their long sentences. That same evening, Maxine declared that, if Pip didn't mind, she wanted to go to Oxford, not California. They could afford it, couldn't they? 'We can afford anything,' Pip said, as Carlotta tuned her cello.

'Your idea presumably,' Wendy said later in the stateroom.

'She envies you,' Victor said.

'I hope you disillusioned her,' Wendy said.

'Of course,' Victor said. 'I disillusion everybody, don't I?'

'Oh Victor,' she said. 'I feel as if I've done you a mischief.'

'Why,' he said, 'what are you planning?'

'Planning?' she said. 'You've got the wrong idea about me. You think I'm a person of serious purposes and educated taste. I'm really much more flippant than you like to think; I'm basically a creature of impulse.'

'Are you really?' he said. 'And whither are you basically impelled at the moment?'

'Curly wants me to come to Hollywood,' she said.

'In what position? I think I can imagine the costume.'

'He thinks I could be in the films,' she said. 'Not that I believe him.'

'Maxine believes him,' Victor said. 'She reckons you're quite the potential star.'

'He needs a personal assistant really,' Wendy said. 'A girl Friday.'

'You'd have the rest of the week to yourself, I presume.'

'Should you mind terribly? The climate sounds so attractive.'

'Mid-summer snowballs, I'm told. What do you mean, should I mind? I'm not going, am I?'

'If you forbid me,' she said, 'I won't either, will I?'

'I don't believe in forbidding people,' Victor said. 'If you haven't got the discrimination to decide these things for yourself, I can scarcely imagine that it would do any good forbidding you. Is he going to pay you for your services or are you giving yourself away?'

'Somewhere or other, Victor, there's a whiff of squalor about you, isn't there?'

'I thought I was behaving with remarkable nobility in the circumstances.'

'I realise that you want me to hurt you,' she said. 'I'm not sure why. But the only way you can express it is by suggesting that I'm not capable of anything except a sort of cheap opportunism.'

'Perhaps that's why you married me,' he said.

'I married you, believe it or not, because I thought you were the most beautiful thing I'd ever seen. I think you find even that rather reprehensible, don't you?'

'You thought I was going to be a success,' he said.

'And aren't you?'

'The world no longer believes that success consists in being underpaid for most of one's life and having a K. and a pension to show for it at the end. The world may well be right, but there isn't much I can do about it now, since I don't possess the means of attracting the attention of Mr Bonaventura. No one buys the film rights of articles in *The Economist* exactly, do they?'

'He thinks you're brilliant, but you do rather intimidate him.'

'He's probably just as clever as I am and he's certainly richer and presumably more attractive.'

'No,' Wendy said, 'just more alive.'

'He's a joke,' Victor said.

'Perhaps I was in need of one. And all I'm taking is a job.'

'And a screen test, I hope. Maxine thinks *I'm* rather droll, as it happens.'

'Maxine! Does she really?'

'Look here, you know what his sort of job implies, don't you, when it comes to bed-time? Just because he's the image of your father, doesn't mean that all he's after is a hand with the groceries, you know.'

'Is that what discrimination means,' Wendy said. 'Sir Victor?'

Maxine went up to Oxford in the following October. The children and their Nanny went with Pip to California. Wendy and the Bonaventuras had gone earlier. They had to find a house for Pip, with the pool and the tennis court. Victor told his friends that his wife was researching for a comparative study of Fitzgerald and Faulkner. If he was lonely, he did not show it. If he was melancholy, he neither moaned nor drank. He went home every evening, with a briefcase full of papers. His work, rather than showing signs of domestic stress, was even more thoroughly argued than before.

When, after her first year's studies, Maxine received à First in Mods, she gave Victor a call. 'You're the only one it means anything to.' She came up to town and they went to the theatre. The play was kindergarten kitsch and they left at the interval. Maxine was slimmer and seemed younger. The maternal puffiness of her face had been refined by careful food (she could afford it) and by the studious régime she had imposed on herself. Her chance had come late and she was determined not to fluff it. Thanks to Pip's generosity, she had lived very comfortably and very quietly. The 'boys' were too young for her. She had a large allowance and she was dressed in an Israeli leather suit and Ferragamo shoes. Her hair had been done by a man in South Molton Street. But what particularly enchanted Victor was her inexhaustible appetite for unparagraphed talk. They went to a restaurant club (Pip's account) and leaned together, discussing Ezra Pound, the

Pisan phase, until they were the last people among the candles. She had taken a room at the Dorchester, where she proposed that they continue their analysis of the relationship between intellectual style and social content, unless he had better things to do. What could be better? He was seduced less by the smart clothes and the markedly smarter accent than by her ravenous interest in his opinions, but the smart clothes were not displeasing and the accent was happier for the Oxford varnish. What was more, she was really rather clever: she listened brilliantly.

It must have been three or four in the morning before anything personal was said, and then it was said quite impersonally: 'I married the wrong woman, you know. I thought that Wendy and I would have conversations like this all our lives, but she never wanted to. All she ever wanted to talk about in the bedroom was bed.'

'I should never have said anything if you hadn't,' Maxine said, 'but of course I *knew* the minute I met her, that night at your house when I was supposed to play the kennel maid. She's lovely, but she's not for you.'

'I had no idea that you had a mind at all at that point,' Victor said. 'I suppose I was a terrible prig, and I still am, I daresay, except that you're not the same person as you were then, are you?'

'Now I'm a prig too,' she said. 'Thanks to Pip. We shouldn't ever forget that.'

'The difficulty,' he said, 'is indeed to know how we ever shall. In spite of everything, I don't relish putting him down yet again, but I suppose we shall have to tell him.'

'Well, in view of what he and Wendy are up to,' Maxine said, 'I don't really see why we should hang back, do you?'

'I'm sorry?'

'Oh Victor,' she said, 'surely you realised?'

'I had the impression that it was the diminutive wop who'd

taken Wendy's passing fancy. You're not telling me it was Pip all the time?'

'Oh Victor, I feel terrible. I thought you knew. I should have known better. Do you mind terribly?'

'Whatever can she see in him?'

'That's not very nice. You are talking about my husband.'

'I'm not under contract to say nice things. You know very well you couldn't ever abide to live with him again. He wouldn't understand a word you were saying. And think of those manuscripts of his, all those bums and titties, you'd never be able to stomach it.'

'Oh Victor,' she said, 'Pip was very decent to me, you know, when I was just a little nobody. And he's always looked up to you. He's always wanted to be something you could be proud of.'

'Look here,' Victor said, 'I've greatly enjoyed our searching analysis of the modern sensibility, but it's no use pretending that there wasn't a sub-text, any more than you took your clothes off in Greece just because the great god Pan happened not to be dead after all, if you had the money. There's obviously been a long-standing case of crossed wires in the Geary family and it's high time it was put right.'

'This is a moment I honestly never dared to hope would come.'

'You should have indicated sooner,' Victor said. 'I suppose the truth is I never really *trusted* Wendy from the moment she turned out not really to be first class. She was beautiful and she was agreeable, but she never began to be the same sort of stuff you are, and I am. When you come to think about it, Pip and she were made for each other.'

'Just like you and I,' Maxine said, pulling the cover off the bed. 'And just think how convenient it is, we shall none of us have to so much as change our names, shall we?'

'Of course,' he said, undoing his belt, 'this is all strictly conditional on you getting a First in your Schools.'